A Hole in the Hedge

A Hole in the Hedge

Grace Casselman

Napoleon Publishing

Toronto, Ontario, Canada

Text © 2003 Grace Casselman

Cover art: James Bentley

Published by Napoleon Publishing/RendezVous Press
Toronto, Ontario, Canada

Le Conseil des Arts du Canada depuis 1957 | The Canada Council for the Arts since 1957

Napoleon Publishing gratefully acknowledges the support of the Canada Council for our publishing program. We also gratefully acknowledge the support of the Government of Ontario through the Ontario Media Development Corporation's Ontario Book Initiative.

Printed in Canada

07 06 05 04 03   5 4 3 2 1

National Library of Canada Cataloguing in Publication

Casselman, Grace, 1969-
    A hole in the hedge / Grace Casselman.

ISBN 0-929141-99-7

I. Title.

PS8555.A7797H64 2003   jC813'.6   C2002-906127-X
PZ7

To my Mother, who taught me how to read.

*And to my husband, Douglas VanderVelde,
who encourages me to write.*

*With thanks to Brian Thompson, who shared
the story of his mother's letter.*

One

The air was heavy, almost damp in the small room, a product of an over-zealous air-conditioner. That machine's soft buzzing was subtle background music, mixing with the low murmurs of hushed voices. A lingering scent from the flower bouquets on and around the polished casket wafted through the thick air. The floral odour was nearly as strong as the questionable perfume the old woman had liberally favoured for most of her eighty-six years.

Mrs. Telgord had lived in the Inglewood area as long as anybody could remember, in a tiny white bungalow with faded yellow curtains. She'd had a soft, quiet demeanour but a bright, friendly smile. The woman was always ready with warm tea and shortbread biscuits for visitors, like the neighbourhood children, the postal carrier and the gas meter reader.

The men and women standing awkwardly about were mainly neighbours, with the exception of one elderly white-haired niece who'd just arrived by train for the wake. She held a faded lace handkerchief and dabbed at the wrinkled corners of her eyes as people murmured their formal condolences before slipping into the back room for coffee.

Twelve-year-old Kaitlin Lora Anderson restlessly shifted in her chair, eyeing the neighbours who'd turned out in their Sunday best. Nobody looked perfectly at ease, not even her dad, who stood making wake-appropriate small talk.

"She was a very hospitable woman," someone whispered. Then: "Well, she lived a good long life." There were nods of heads and general murmurs of agreement. Someone, probably Mrs. Peters from across the road, piped up with: "She grew beautiful geraniums." There was a moment of complete silence, until Kaitlin's dad kindly agreed: "Why yes, she certainly did."

Kaitlin tugged impatiently at her socks. One seemed to have lost its elasticity and kept slipping down to her ankles. She sighed and turned down the edges a couple of times, then pushed the socks right down, deliberately bunching them. "Funeral fashion," she thought, wondering for the thirty-second time if it had been a bad idea to wear a purple dress to a funeral home.

She'd wanted to buy a black dress, but her dad said it wasn't necessary, that people didn't really wear black to funerals or wakes these days. That seemed to be true, as only Mrs. Peters was totally dressed in black, and Mrs. Telgord's body wore a yellow dress with white flowers.

Kaitlin glanced covertly at the casket. She felt uneasy about being so close to a dead body and literally jumped when her father put his hand on her shoulder. "Katie." He smiled at her gently. "You can go up and look at Mrs. Telgord. Go say goodbye." She nodded and carefully stepped up to the front of the room.

It was undeniably Mrs. Telgord lying there, but somehow she didn't look quite right. Her eyes were closed, but she was wearing her glasses. Kaitlin wondered why the woman really needed her glasses now.

Someone had put makeup on her, making her face look darker than usual, and her lips and cheeks were redder than they'd ever been in life. Her white hands were primly folded across her chest.

Kaitlin felt a touch on the top of her head, as Reverend Brown came up beside her. "This is just a shell, Kaitlin," he said softly. "Mrs. Telgord is already in heaven." The minister smiled. "I bet she's having a wonderful time right now." He patted Kaitlin benignly on the shoulder, then moved on to speak to the niece.

Kaitlin frowned.

She looked back at the room, but the adults seemed engrossed in their conversations. She pressed her stomach close to the side of the casket and very discreetly reached out to touch the back of Mrs. Telgord's hand. The skin didn't feel quite real. It was very cool, almost like plastic.

Kaitlin stared intensely at the closed eyes. Mrs. Telgord always made chocolate brownies on Thursdays, she thought irrelevantly. And then she remembered going to Mrs. Telgord to get a knee bandaged up after a failed skateboarding experiment.

She felt something burning under her eyelids. She shook her head and concentrated. "Wake up," she willed, squinting her eyes, aiming the thought very hard at Mrs. Telgord's body. "Please. Get up now."

But nothing happened.

Kaitlin sighed deeply.

"I saw you touch her," an amused voice said, just behind her.

It was Michael Drayson, the hated boy from next door. He was particularly groomed today, his usually unruly sandy-brown hair parted and combed flat. He was wearing a white shirt and even a tie.

I bet it's just a clip-on. I should pull it right off him, Kaitlin thought uncharitably. Instead, she just scowled at him. "Go away."

He opened his eyes wide at her, with a touch of a smile. "Always nice to see you too." His expression grew more sombre as he stared at Mrs. Telgord. He glanced back at Kaitlin, then walked silently off.

Kaitlin looked at Mrs. Telgord's closed eyes under the glasses. "Boys," she said, imagining the older woman smiling back at that. But instead, this face was perfectly expressionless.

There was a weird feeling in Kaitlin's stomach, like fingers gripping her insides. She wondered if, seven years ago, her mother had lain so still in her coffin. She wondered if they'd put too much make-up on her and whether or not she'd been buried wearing her reading glasses.

Kaitlin started to cry. At first it was slow tears rolling down her cheeks, then quiet sobs made her shoulders shake.

"Katie," her dad said, appearing quickly beside her. He put a hand on her shoulder. He handed her a bunch of tissue and patted her on the back. "Go on outside, dear. I'll be right out."

She wiped at her face with the tissue and tried to breathe more normally. Around her, she could hear people whispering: "Poor girl, she's so sensitive." and "She must have been very close to the deceased."

Of course, Mrs. Peters had to make a comment. "Children don't belong at funerals," she whispered, but so loudly that everyone heard.

Kaitlin ignored them all. "Goodbye, Mrs. Telgord," she said, very softly. "I'll miss you."

She rubbed the already damp tissue against her wet cheek and ran out the door.

*   *   *

In the car, Kaitlin and her dad rode in silence. He eyed her speculatively once or twice before pulling into a drive-through ice cream place. At the window, he ordered two double-scoop chocolate cones. Her dad always insisted that love of chocolate is one of those genetic traits. "Here, Katie," he said, handing her the cone. "I'm glad you came along with me today. I hope it wasn't too rough on you."

Kaitlin shrugged, licking slowly at her ice cream. "Dad?"

"Hmm?" he answered, licking a chocolate drip off the cone a split-second before it would have dropped onto his clean white shirt.

She kept her eyes on her ice cream. "Why didn't you let me see Mom after she died?"

"Oh, sweetie." He paused and looked at her for a long moment. "You were very young, just five years old.

You were already so upset about her cancer." His voice was sad. "It seemed best for you not to go to the funeral. I thought it would be too upsetting. I wanted you to remember your Mom when she was alive."

Kaitlin didn't say anything. She bit loudly into her cone to fill the silence, even though she wasn't very hungry. She wondered if her father would say more. She glanced sideways at his face. At first he looked like he would, but then he didn't.

Her dad finished off his cone just as he pulled into the driveway, but Kaitlin carried hers inside.

Kaitlin's four-year-old half-sister Anna let out a howl of envy and outrage at the sight of the ice cream.

"Oh, Daniel," sighed Jane, the evil stepmother, peering into the living room. "So close to dinner?"

Kaitlin smiled to herself at the havoc. She ran upstairs to her room while her father joined Jane in the kitchen, talking about the wake and Mrs. Telgord's niece.

"Kaitlin, will you please wash up and set the table?" Jane called out as she bustled about the kitchen, peeling and chopping various nutrition-packed vegetables. Kaitlin pretended not to hear as she shut the door behind her.

"Kaitlin!" Jane called, more loudly, no doubt sending an exasperated look towards her husband.

"Oh, let her be. It's been a rough day for her. I'll help you."

Suppressing momentary guilt, Kaitlin pulled off the defective socks. She decided to go barefoot and slipped into her favourite jeans and an over-sized purple T-shirt.

She remembered shopping for the garment with Jane. "Do you have it in purple?" Jane had asked. "My daughter's going through a purple stage."

"Stepdaughter," Kaitlin had reminded her in alarm. Jane had sighed but bought the shirt anyway. Kaitlin frowned at the memory.

Jane had married Kaitlin's father just two years after Kaitlin's mother had died. Her stepmother was tall and thin and energetic, with very straight ash-coloured hair that hung just past her shoulders. She was a corporate attorney and supposedly a good one. That's what the other lawyers would tell Kaitlin when they came to dinner. "Your mom's a great lawyer, kid," they'd say.

"Stepmother," she'd correct. "And my name's Kaitlin." Then she'd scowl at them until they gave up the attempt at conversation.

Kaitlin knew she didn't make it easy for her stepmother, but then again, that was the goal. Although her dad sternly required perfect politeness to Jane, Kaitlin preferred to achieve that with the least possible warmth. She stared at her own green-eyed reflection in the mirror. She picked up a brush and dragged it impatiently through her dark hair. Since she was young, she'd liked to pretend her reflection was her identical twin. So she'd talk to the girl in the mirror, dubbed a more glamourous "Katerina."

"It's not that Jane is truly evil," Kaitlin told Katerina solemnly, "but she's an intruder. She has to understand that she's not truly wanted here. That's our job," she admonished her reflection.

The door to her bedroom nudged open, and a small four-year-old face peeked in. The bright blue eyes were nearly obscured by blonde ringlets. The hair tended to bounce as the little girl jumped about. "Who are you talking to?" Anna asked, wide-eyed.

"Never mind. Why didn't you knock before opening the door, like I've told you?" She made her most horrible face at the girl, crossing her eyes, baring her teeth and sticking out her tongue all at once.

Anna shrugged cheerfully but eyed Kaitlin with interest. "I forgot." Her words slurred, because she was sucking on the ear of a raggedy teddy bear. She gazed about Kaitlin's room with curiosity, as if she hadn't seen it before. "Messy, messy," she taunted.

Kaitlin intensified the ferocity of her grimace, but her half-sister only giggled through a mouthful of bear's ear.

"Mrs. Telgord went to heaven." Anna beamed with the information. "Mommy told me."

"I know that."

"I hope she comes back soon," said Anna, her chubby fingers reaching towards the lace apron of Kaitlin's favourite china doll, who was leaning daintily against a pillow.

"Don't touch that," said Kaitlin automatically. She picked up the doll herself, to keep it out of danger. Then she squinted. "What do you mean? Mrs. Telgord isn't coming back."

"Yes, she is. 'Cause she promised."

"What?" Kaitlin peered down into Anna's bright gaze.

"She promised to make me brownies, and Mrs. Telgord wouldn't forget."

Kaitlin stared at her half-sister for a moment. "No, Mrs. Telgord wouldn't forget."

Two

Kaitlin sat looking out into the street, entwined in the old wooden fence at the edge of her lawn. She rested her chin on her crossed arms and leaned against the fence's top board, sitting a bit precariously on a lower section of fencing. Her legs dangled.

She kicked lightly at a stray dandelion protected by a fence post from her Dad's indifferent mowing. It bobbed good-naturedly. A bee buzzed in the near-distance. Kaitlin gave it her most daunting frown, and it flitted away.

"Even bugs are scared of you," a voice intruded. "I bet you never even need to wear bug repellent."

Michael stood on his own lawn, leaning over his mother's cedar hedge as he balanced a basketball on the rather uneven branches, rolling it slightly back and forth.

"I wish I was wearing it *now*," she replied, lifting an eyebrow pointedly at him.

He laughed, shaking his head. He threw the ball just slightly into the air. "You look kind of pitiful sitting there by yourself. Did you chase away all your friends?"

Kaitlin glared at him, tossing her head so her hair flew behind her. "I don't see any gang of friends hanging around you. Speak for yourself."

Grinning, Michael held up his basketball. "Hey, I'm on my way to collect my gang now!"

The sight of a brown sedan driving slowly up the road distracted Kaitlin. The tires crunched over gravel as the car turned into her own driveway. She waved a hand dismissively at Michael. "Well, see you." She turned her back to him.

"Hey, is that your friend Tracy?" he asked, undaunted, leaning over the hedge a bit farther. "Maybe I'll stick around and say hello."

"Go away *now*," she hissed unyieldingly.

"Yes, ma'am," he replied, insolently obedient. He strolled off whistling, spinning the basketball on a fingertip.

"Show-off," Kaitlin murmured under her breath.

Tracy Leeland, Kaitlin's very best friend in the whole world, climbed up onto the fence beside her. "He's pretty good at basketball, you know."

The dark-haired girl was petite and nearly half-a-head shorter than Kaitlin. She sidled closer to Kaitlin, and they took turns kicking at the dandelion. They giggled when they missed the flower and accidentally kicked each other.

"Blech," said Kaitlin in regards to Michael. She screwed up her face until Tracy burst out laughing.

"Oh, stop it." Tracy tossed her long black ponytail, rolling her eyes. "Why are you so mean to him?"

"He started it," Kaitlin replied, but refused to elaborate.

Once, she and Michael had been nearly inseparable.

As toddlers, they used to slip through the hole in the hedge and go in search of one another. Their favourite activities were jumping through puddles, collecting rocks, sticks and bugs, and playing with an occasional neighbourhood pet.

Their families had been close too. Kaitlin's father and Ben Drayson had studied civil engineering together at university. After they'd graduated, they'd become business partners and had started up a small company that specialized in the structures of small office buildings. The kids' mothers had been good friends too.

Kaitlin had cried as if her heart were breaking the day that Michael, nearly one year older, had gone off to kindergarten alone. But at three o'clock every afternoon, she'd slip through the hedge to head over to Mrs. Drayson's kitchen, awaiting his return. Then Michael would proudly describe his day, and Kaitlin would exclaim dutifully over the magazine cutouts, the crayon drawings and the various other wonders of "school."

The next autumn, Michael, as self-appointed chaperone and tour-guide, walked her to and from the schoolyard, offering hints and tips on avoiding naptime and optimizing craft opportunities while maximizing snack breaks. And once, when a bully had pulled Kaitlin's hair and made her cry, Michael had punched him in the nose, then held the big boy down so Kaitlin could punch him too.

Those were the good old days. But Kaitlin had sworn never to forgive Michael for the day when he'd publicly shunned her. She'd been eight years old. She'd seen a bunch of the Grade Four boys playing catch and strolled over to join in, confident of a customary welcome.

The group had laughed and told her to go back to the "little girls", but she'd held her head high, looking to Michael for support.

But it hadn't come.

He'd only glanced at her and mumbled, "This is a boys' game, kid," before turning away from her and tossing the ball to one of the others.

She'd stood there in shock, certain he would change his mind, or come over and apologize. But he hadn't. He'd just ignored her and kept on playing. And it didn't matter that it had happened four years ago. It was an unbearable slight, Kaitlin reminded herself. Michael didn't deserve to be her friend. And who cared if he knew how to twirl a basketball?

Tracy kicked her lightly on the shin, interrupting the reverie.

"Ouch!" Kaitlin frowned.

"He's getting kind of cute, don't you think?"

"Certainly not," Kaitlin replied, grimacing. "Ew. Double ew."

"And he's getting taller," Tracy continued. "He might be the tallest in the school even."

"Stop it," Kaitlin said crossly. "If you get a crush on Michael Drayson, I will kill you." She paused. "I will mess up your hair, and *then* I'll kill you."

Tracy held up her palms in the air in mock surrender, before she started to fall backwards and had to grab onto the fence again for support. Both girls burst out in a fit of laughter.

"Besides," said Tracy, gasping a bit, still laughing,

"he's got a girlfriend."

"What? He does not."

"He does," Tracy insisted with a vigorous nod. "He's dating Shelley Whitfield. You know, she's in his Grade Eight class, the cheerleader with the curly blonde ponytail. She's always yelling *his* name at the basketball games," Tracy said, rolling her eyes.

"Bah. She's annoying."

Tracy nodded. "I think so, too. He should like *you*."

Kaitlin slapped her friend on the arm, not very lightly. "Don't insult me like that."

Grinning, Tracy rubbed her arm. "What? What? What did I say?"

"Is she really his girlfriend?" Kaitlin asked, but nonchalantly, as if she didn't particularly care.

"Definitely. Everyone's talking about it."

"Michael's not old enough to have a girlfriend," frowned Kaitlin. She paused, looking for something more insightful to add. Then, in a voice that brooked no argument, she finished: "And he's stupid. That poor girl."

*   *   *

They lay on the floor of Kaitlin's bedroom, staring at the ceiling.

"Well," Tracy said, "I think it's cool, although maybe a bit creepy. What does your mom say?"

"Stepmother," corrected Kaitlin automatically. Then she turned and flashed a smile at Tracy. "It was her idea." Kaitlin tilted her head, thinking about that. "Well," she expanded, "it was her idea to get the stuffed animals off the floor by hanging them from the ceiling. I'm not sure if she wanted me to tie the ropes around their necks like that or not."

Kaitlin shrugged, casually eyeing the bears, pigs, snakes, rabbits, kangaroos and birds that comprised her rather comprehensive collection of stuffed toys. "Jane says she likes it. My Dad doesn't care, but he nearly had a heart attack when he walked in here in the dark to say goodnight to me, and a bunch of animals banged him on the head. Jane made me shorten the ropes a little after that."

The girls grinned at each other. "Besides," Kaitlin continued with a lofty wave upwards, "after you stuck the glow-in-the-dark solar system all over your ceiling, I realized mine was sadly under-decorated."

"I bet we have the coolest ceilings in Grade Seven," boasted Tracy. Then she sighed. "We need to invite more people over, so word will get around."

"Naw. But we do need to carry more props."

"Props?"

Kaitlin waved her arms about expressively. "*Props.* We need something to make ourselves seem extra-cool. It has to be something different, something that stands out. We want to make a statement."

"Like costumes?"

"Well," said Kaitlin mischievously, "long capes might do it."

Tracy looked alarmed. Kaitlin tossed a pillow at her. "I'm kidding, silly. We don't want to be weird. We've got to pick the perfect thing." She looked about the room, thinking. "Like, we could both dress only in one colour."

"We already mostly wear purple," Tracy interjected. "We could wear white gloves." She stretched out her arm and wiggled her fingers playfully.

But Kaitlin shot that down. "That would be too prissy." She pursed her lips, pondering the matter. "Maybe a hat would do." She disappeared into the depths of her closet for a moment, then reappeared, obviously dissatisfied. "I'll be right back," she said. She went out into the hall closet and rooted through the assortment of caps and hats.

Her evil stepmother appeared in the hallway. "What are you looking for, Kaitlin?" she inquired mildly.

Kaitlin scowled. "I want to start wearing a hat."

"A baseball cap?"

"No, no, no. It has to be something more unique, yet particularly cool."

Jane smiled slightly, pausing in contemplation. "I might have something that could work. Give me a second."

Kaitlin nodded and went back into her bedroom. Tracy was fiddling with the clothing on the china doll, but Kaitlin didn't say anything. Tracy *was* her best friend, after all.

There was a gentle knock at the door. Kaitlin waited a few seconds before taking a deep breath and calling out grandly, "You may come in!"

Jane opened the door, smiling at both of them. "Hi, Tracy."

"Hi, Mrs. Anderson," said Tracy, smiling back.

"Oh, Tracy," the stepmother replied, "you know you can call me Jane, like Kaitlin does. How are you doing?"

"Oh, I'm fine, Jane," Tracy replied sweetly, stressing the name. "How are you?"

Kaitlin frowned at all the pleasantness.

"I'm fine, too, thank you," said Jane, handing a straw hat to Kaitlin. "Might this possibly work? You can keep it, if you want it."

Kaitlin took the hat and examined it carefully. It didn't look like a farmer's hat, and the brim was just about the right width. Ideally, it would be most satisfying to spurn Jane's help, but Kaitlin thought she'd better try the hat on first. She regarded her reflection critically in the mirror. She pulled down one side of the hat, so it sat a bit jauntily on her head. *Oh, Katerina, it's perfect!* Kaitlin thought.

Tracy, the ideal best friend, unwittingly echoed the sentiment. "It's so you, Kaitlin. I really like it."

As Kaitlin preened a bit, Jane smiled, then slipped out of the room.

"Don't hate me," whispered Tracy, glancing about guiltily, "but I kind of like her."

Kaitlin shrugged and made one of her particularly disdainful faces. "Whatever. Just don't forget you're on my side."

Tracy dramatically crossed her heart. "I won't." She sat up suddenly. "Hey! What's my prop going to be?"

Kaitlin looked her best friend over. "I suppose you could have a hat too."

"Naw, hats make me feel like an umbrella."

Kaitlin giggled in spite of herself. "That's a horrible thing to say, after I've just decided on a hat for my prop."

"Oh, I didn't mean that. Hats look great on you. Say,

could I borrow something of yours, to use as my prop?"

"I guess so. What did you have it mind?"

Tracy opened her eyes wide and gave Kaitlin her sweetest-ever smile. "Fred."

Kaitlin looked up at the tiny brown stuffed beagle hanging from the ceiling. "You want a stuffed toy to be your prop?"

"Not just any toy," said Tracy. "Fred. He's just so cute and little. I could have him sticking out of my backpack, or just carry him around, or put him on the corner of my desk. I could put a leash on him and pretend he's a real dog."

Although she was a bit reluctant to give up her possession, Kaitlin nodded slowly. "It might work..."

Tracy positively beamed as Kaitlin released the noose around Fred's neck. "It'll be great."

Three

The sun radiated over the dark asphalt. Biting delicately into a celery stick, Kaitlin tossed her detested carrots over to Tracy, who in turn paused to give Fred a bite.

Tracy is destined to be an actress, Kaitlin mused, watching her petite friend hold court to a small crowd of Grade Seven kids.

"No, no, no," admonished Tracy archly, slapping lightly at one boy's hand. "Fred gets very nervous around strangers. You have to wait until you're properly introduced. You can pet him only when I say so."

"Uh, sorry," stuttered the red-headed kid named Chuck. He flushed to his equally red hairline and quickly withdrew his hand.

Tracy gave him a quick, subtle wink, and Chuck smiled then blushed again.

Clearing her throat, she continued. "Now, very well. This is my dog Fred, a gift from my dear friend Kaitlin." She clasped her hands over her heart for a moment, turning to Kaitlin, pantomiming extreme gratitude.

"My pleasure, darling," Kaitlin drawled, tipping her hat in mock seriousness.

Tracy feigned a half-curtsy and resumed her seat on the school step. "Fred is an extremely loyal dog, ready and willing to attack anyone who even looks at me sideways." She fixed all her listeners with a stern, warning look. "If you haven't been properly introduced, you'd better keep your distance. Fred has been known to bite, and I can't answer for the consequences."

Rolling her eyes, Kaitlin grinned as the boys took a step backwards, pretending to be afraid.

"Man, she cracks me up," chuckled Winter Carter-Jones, sliding down beside Kaitlin. Winter leaned over and helped herself to one of the offending carrots that Tracy was neglecting in the excitement of her performance. Winter was Kaitlin's second-best friend. She had rich brown skin and short, curly black hair, which was usually decorated with ribbons and tiny braids. Today, she was wearing a bright green miniskirt, purple tights and an orange pull-over. Winter was widely considered to be the trend-setter of the seventh grade.

A second carrot disappeared, and Tracy gasped in mock-horror. She frowned at Winter, who was chewing nonchalantly on the evidence. "Those belong to Fred, and he bites when he's angry."

"So I hear," Winter replied cheerfully. "But I can take a little dog like that."

Fred emitted a low growl, or more accurately a helpful supporter in the audience did.

"There, there," said Tracy, as she petted the little stuffed dog. "It's okay, Fred. Winter's bark is worse than her bite."

Kaitlin nearly choked on her celery. Winter pounded

her on the back. "I'd suggest," Winter responded, "avoiding both my bark and my bite."

Tracy turned her back, ignoring Winter for the moment.

Leaning over to Kaitlin, Winter whispered: "Tracy never brings a lunch any more. Did you notice?"

Kaitlin shrugged.

Winter paused for a moment, contemplating. Then she cleared her throat loudly to get Tracy's attention again, before reaching into her knapsack. She pulled out a bright red apple. "I don't suppose Fred would covet this?"

"Why yes," said Tracy, pacified. "He would." She slipped the fruit into a pocket. "Now, I'm going to introduce Fred to Chuck, and then Ashley is going to take Fred for a walk." She ruffled the fur on the little dog's head. "Fred, this is Chuck. He's an okay guy, so don't bite him, if you can help yourself." She smiled sweetly up at Chuck, instructing: "You can pet him, but do it very carefully. And don't move too fast."

Chuck blushed again, and a couple of his friends snickered. But he bravely reached out to pet the bad-tempered little beast on the nose.

Winter burst out laughing. Quickly, Chuck slunk away with his pals. Tracy carefully tied Fred's leash to his collar and lifted the dog into Ashley Johnson's arms. "You can walk him, but don't go anywhere where I can't see you," Tracy instructed.

Eager for the responsibility, Ashley nodded and followed the instructions.

Frowning suspiciously at Winter, Tracy retrieved the

apple and started munching away, keeping an eye on Fred and Ashley. The pale blonde girl walked about the schoolyard with the little dog in her arms, murmuring to it.

"That kid will do whatever you guys tell her to, won't she?" Winter chortled.

"That's why we keep her around," Tracy whispered back.

Kaitlin interceded. "Naw, she just likes to be involved in the *antics*." She and Winter were very competitive about showing off their vocabularies.

"Antics, hmm?" repeated Winter dryly. "*Shenanigans*, I'd say. Or, *capers*."

Kaitlin opened her mouth, trying furiously to come up with a better synonym, but she was spared the effort when her precious straw hat was suddenly snatched off her head.

"Keeping off the rain, Kaitlin?" inquired a voice that was surprisingly deep for Grade Seven.

Glenn Waters twirled the hat lightly, just out of reach. He was a tall, handsome boy, with wavy brown hair and teasing eyes. He was bigger than most of the guys, probably because he was already thirteen years old. Rumour said he had been held back in Grade Three, but nobody knew for sure. He'd just moved to the area with his mom after his parents' divorce.

Kaitlin didn't know Glenn very well. He was fairly popular overall, but he didn't seem to really fit tightly into any particular group of friends. Sometimes he hung out with Chuck and his friends, sometimes with the basketball team. On occasion, he'd even disappear behind the school with the so-called "wild" kids who usually smelled faintly of smoke.

She resisted the urge to grab the hat out of his hands, knowing it was likely a futile effort that would detract from her dignity. Instead she leaned back against the step. Putting on an amused tone, she said, "I didn't know you cared."

He lifted an eyebrow at her, looking her over for a moment. "Maybe I do. Maybe I just want the hat." And he strolled off.

"Don't worry," said Winter. "He'll bring it back."

"Yeah."

"At least, he probably will," Winter amended as the bell rang and the kids swarmed back to class. Kaitlin grumbled to herself, gathering up her books before the incoming crowd trampled them.

As the kids pushed up the steps, Kaitlin felt the hat settle back onto her head. Glenn passed her, but he turned back and gave her a slow smile before disappearing into the school.

Winter jabbed Kaitlin lightly in the ribs.

Tracy giggled and whispered, "He's so cute."

Kaitlin blushed and reached up to push the hat tighter onto her head.

"Kaitlin's got an admirer," mocked Michael, appearing suddenly. Shelley Whitfield was tightly gripping his elbow, laughing at the wit of Michael's remark.

Kaitlin gave him her best look of utter contempt and marched inside.

*   *   *

Opening the door to her bedroom, Kaitlin stopped suddenly. Her gaze was drawn immediately to the centre of the room. Almost instinctively, she let out a fearsome scream.

Startled, Anna jumped to her feet and screamed too.

The china doll lay naked on the floor. Delicate lace and silk garments were strewn about the room, in complete disarray. Kaitlin gasped in pure outrage. She gathered up steam and ran straight at her half-sister with her arms over her head, in her most frightening fierce monster imitation. Anna shrieked in terror intermixed with giggles, then ducked and dashed about the room, employing well-worn evasion tactics.

Kaitlin wasn't sure what she'd do when she caught the girl. But quick footsteps in the hall soon produced the evil stepmother. "Whatever is going on?" she asked, slightly breathless.

"Look!" Kaitlin exclaimed, pointing in righteous indignation at the outrage to her doll, lying exposed on the floor. "Just *look* at that!"

Anna was still shrieking and running about in tiny hyperactive circles. Her hands waved in the air while her blonde curls bounced frantically.

"Shush, Anna. Stop that. Motor over to your own bedroom, and keep quiet for a while," commanded Jane.

The child complied, tapping each foot double-time, humming her best four-year-old train imitation as she headed out the door.

"A moment, young lady," Jane interrupted her. "What did I say about playing with Kaitlin's toys?"

"Bermission!" Anna recalled, wide-eyed, still double-stepping. "Ask for bermission!"

Jane nodded, resting her hand lightly on Anna's shoulder to slow the locomotion. "Yes, permission. Did you ask for Kaitlin's permission to play with her doll?"

Anna's bottom lip quivered in her downcast face. "I forgot."

Kaitlin sniffed.

Jane regarded her small daughter for a moment longer. "Apologize to your sister, Anna."

Adopting a pitiful expression, Anna lifted her mournful eyes to Kaitlin. "Sowwy, sowwy," she pleaded.

Kaitlin scowled.

Jane pushed Anna gently out the door. "Go play in your room until dinner, please."

The train started up again, chug-chug-chugging down the hall.

Jane leaned down and picked up the doll, smoothing the sadly disarranged curls lightly. She flipped it over, looking for damage. Finding none, she gathered up the undergarments, petticoats, blouse, skirt, socks and shoes, turning them right-side out. She handed the doll and clothes to Kaitlin. "I don't think there's any permanent harm."

Kaitlin screwed up her face, unconvinced. "If these dolls get messed with too much, they're never the same. This is a collector's item, you know."

"I know. She's just fascinated with the pretty clothes, I think."

Kaitlin squinted unforgivingly. "It's just lucky I arrived when I did." She let her face settle into its familiar frown lines.

Heavy steps in the hallway announced the arrival of her dad. His reading glasses were propped on the top of his head. His shirt was partly unbuttoned, and his sleeves were rolled up. "I was studying some plans when I heard some terrible screaming. Eventually, I realized I ought to investigate." He grinned at Jane, as if they shared some private joke.

Kaitlin rolled her eyes. She put the doll down on the bed, carefully laying out the clothes to hide the nakedness as best as possible. Even dolls deserve some decency, after all.

She clasped her hands tightly together and fell on the floor dramatically at her dad's knees. "Please, Dad, please, please. Help me. I need more privacy. I need protection for my stuff. I need sanctuary."

She laid her cheek alongside the back of her clasped hands, acting out the plea.

Her father seemed a bit startled. He looked back and forth from her to Jane in perplexity.

"Dad, I'm begging you. I need a lock. I always ask her to knock, and to stay out of my room when I'm not here, but she never does. Please, please…"

"I don't know," he said slowly. "Sometimes we need to get into this room. And we need to be able to vacuum in here. And what if there's a fire? I'd need to be able to get to you."

Kaitlin moaned.

"Well, Daniel," Jane interjected practically, "we have a lock on our bedroom door, after all."

"I'm aware of that." He flashed her a warm look.

Kaitlin grimaced. But still, her dad appeared to be

wavering. "Please, Dad? Double, triple please?"

"Well, I suppose I could get some sort of slide lock for privacy when you're in the room," he said. He glanced again at Jane, who nodded gently.

"I'm sure you could kick it open easily, if there was a fire, Daniel. I think that would be fine."

Kaitlin giggled at the prospect of her father kicking down a door.

"What?" he asked, mildly insulted. "I work out."

But Jane was smiling too, so Kaitlin quickly resumed a more sullen expression.

"What you really need," said her stepmother, "is a lockable cupboard of some sort, a place to put your valuables. Daniel, didn't you just say you'd like to get back into your wood-working?"

"Umm. I might have said that in a moment of weakness."

"Nonsense," Jane continued briskly. "I'm sure you meant it."

"I probably did, at the time." But he nodded. "Okay, I'll get working on that. First the lock, then the cupboard."

Kaitlin looked at him, still a bit doubtful.

"I promise!" he insisted. He squeezed Kaitlin's shoulder and gazed into her eyes with an exclusively warm smile. A feeling of happiness expanded inside her chest, but then her father took his wife's hand to escort her out of the room. Kaitlin was annoyed. She reached over to the door, intending to shut them out.

She wasn't quick enough to avoid seeing her father pull her evil stepmother into a close hug and press a light kiss onto her mouth.

Kaitlin slammed the door. The swoosh of resulting air caused the stuffed animals hanging from the ceiling to swing lightly back and forth.

After redressing the china doll, Kaitlin lay down on the bed, hugging the small figure close, all the while careful not to mess up the delicate ringlets. Lying very still, she sighed deeply. She turned her gaze to the ceiling. A small pink rabbit with long droopy ears swayed slowly, just above her pillow.

*   *   *

True to his word, Dad arrived the next day to install a lock on her door, armed with drills, screws, hammers and nails. Anna looked on, her expression mournful. Feeling generous, Kaitlin smiled almost sweetly at her half-sister, who would soon be safely barred on the other side of the door.

"Is Mrs. Telgord back?" Anna asked hopefully.

"She's not coming back. I told you that."

"She is! She's baking me brownies, she said," Anna insisted. Her face screwed up, and she looked like she was going to cry.

"Have an apple," Kaitlin suggested dryly. Anna shook her head vigorously and stomped off.

*   *   *

Outside, the sky was dark, with heavy clouds rumbling overhead. Mrs. Drayson was clipping determinedly at the hedge. "Oh, Katie!" she exclaimed in pleasure. "How are you?"

Kaitlin had always adored her neighbour, despite that misfortune in sons, otherwise known as Michael. Mrs. Drayson was slim, with curly waist-length hair that was the same shade of light brown as Michael's. And she had the same deep grey eyes.

"I'm okay. How are you?"

"I'm great," said Mrs. Drayson, beaming at her.

Suddenly Kaitlin stared closely at the hedge. "Hey. Do you *cut* that hole in there?"

Mrs. Drayson looked embarrassed. "Well, let's say I trim it. You guys used to scrape yourselves going through, so I started trimming it."

"Yes, but..." Kaitlin paused, in confusion, "but we don't use it any more."

"Oh, I know," Mrs. Drayson sighed. "Maybe I'm just sentimental." She gave Kaitlin a mischievous glance. "Or hopeful."

Kaitlin shook her head, perplexed. "Plus, we're old enough to walk around on the sidewalk now."

"I know. You kids are certainly growing up fast. I can hardly believe it." She shook her head, smiling. "Say, would you like to come over now?"

Thinking of Michael, Kaitlin shuddered. "I'd better not."

"Are you sure? I'm all alone here, and I'd love to show you my latest paintings."

Kaitlin hesitated.

"I've got chocolate-chip cookies."

Laughing, Kaitlin nodded. "How can I resist?" She

squeezed through the hole in the hedge, for old times' sake.

Inside, Mrs. Drayson showed her some small easels filled with pretty water-sketches of wild flowers. They were light, happy scenes, with dancing pastel colours showing tender landscapes. She sold the small paintings to local art shops and a few greeting-card makers. "You should paint with me sometimes, like you used to."

"I hate being so bad at it."

"What?" exclaimed Mrs. Drayson. "I've always thought you were very talented."

"Not like you," Kaitlin protested. It had actually been fun, painting with her neighbour.

"You wouldn't have been very impressed with my work when I was young. It takes practice, dear. But if you like painting, you should definitely keep it up."

Kaitlin dipped her cookie into her milk. Some crumbs broke off immediately. "Mrs. Drayson?"

"Yes, Katie?"

"Was my mother your best friend?"

The woman paused for a moment, breaking a chocolate chip off her own cookie. "I always think of my husband Ben as my best friend, you know."

"But of your women friends?"

"I think so, yes. Your Mom was probably my best friend. She was terribly sweet, you know."

"Sometimes I'm afraid I'm forgetting her," Kaitlin admitted softly. "Mostly, I just remember her being in the hospital."

Mrs. Drayson gave Kaitlin a concerned look. "Oh, honey. It was rough at the end, with your mother so very sick. But even then, she was a very special woman." She paused. "I remember how she used to laugh. It was nearly musical. Her laughter was so beautiful. Contagious too. I used to leave her hospital room smiling. It seems so odd to remember that, but that's how your mom was, dear. She warmed the people around her."

Ignoring the tears pricking her eyes, Kaitlin took an extra-big gulp of milk. "You're not really friends with Jane, are you?"

Mrs. Drayson smiled slightly. "Don't ask me to compare them, dear. You shouldn't either. Jane is a very nice woman, and she's wonderful for your father. But she's gone at the office all day, and in the evenings we're both busy with our families, so we don't get a lot of time to visit."

"Why did he have to get married again?" Kaitlin whispered the question.

Mrs. Drayson shook her head. "Your dad was so lonely, Katie. And he met Jane, and they fell in love."

Kaitlin grimaced.

Mrs. Drayson continued. "It doesn't mean he doesn't love your mom any more. He's just going on with his life. Your mother would have wanted that."

Kaitlin shook her head, unconvinced. Just then, there was a loud clatter at the door. Michael and his father burst in, shaking off water.

"Oh, dear," said Mrs. Drayson. "It's raining, I see. Close the door before we all get drenched!"

Michael looked surprised to see who was in his kitchen. "Hey, Kaitlin," he said, leaning his umbrella against the wall.

Kaitlin jumped to her feet in dismay. "Hi, Mr. Drayson," she said pointedly to Michael's father. "Mrs. Drayson, thank you for the milk. I'd better get home. Someone might be looking for me."

Looking a bit disappointed, the woman nodded. "Okay, Katie. Please come back soon."

Her husband's eyes twinkled at the sight of Kaitlin as he squeezed past Michael. "Kaitlin!" he boomed in his big jovial voice. He reached into his jacket pocket and pulled out a candy in a shiny wrapper. "Look what I've been carrying around just for you!" he exclaimed.

Kaitlin grinned, accepting the candy. He always had some treats secreted in one pocket or another. It made him extra-popular with kids. "Thank you, Mr. Drayson."

"No, no, thank you. It was getting heavy. I'm glad you finally came by to take it off my hands!"

"Oh, Ben," Mrs. Drayson laughed, shaking her head. "You're incorrigible." She reached up and kissed his cheek.

"Just the way you like me," he returned, giving his wife a squeeze.

Kaitlin brushed past Michael on her way out. "Do you want to borrow an umbrella?" he asked her quietly. "It's raining pretty hard."

"I'd rather drown," she hissed.

Lifting her head haughtily, she stepped into the rain.

Four

Big fat drops of rain rolled slowly down the classroom window, forming perfect tears on the pane of glass. Kaitlin watched in silent wonder as a droplet travelled carefully, almost delicately on its exquisite journey, eventually smashing into nothingness on the outside windowsill.

Kaitlin sighed. She should have been used to the mindless destruction of raindrops. It had been pouring for days.

Reluctantly, she turned her attention back indoors, where Ms. Manon was writing an assignment on the board. The chalk squealed in protest at the teacher's vigorous strokes. Kaitlin dutifully recorded the page numbers into her notebook while cringing at the sound.

Instead of launching into a Social Studies lesson, the teacher said she was going to read a story to the class.

Kaitlin leaned back in her chair. She loved hearing stories read aloud. Ms. Manon's firm voice was nicely punctuated by the rushing and rumbling of the stormy day.

The teacher was insistent on being called Ms., not Miss or Mrs. She wasn't quite conventional, but she was very popular with her class. Ms. Manon always encouraged the kids to think about things like stereotypes and gender roles. Why shouldn't boys play with dolls if they wanted? And why shouldn't girls play with toy trains? And she applauded when Winter confessed to wanting to be an astronaut when she grew up.

Kaitlin wasn't surprised when the teacher began reading her chosen story. It was about a little girl who moved to a new school where little boys wore pants, and little girls wore skirts or dresses. But this little girl in the story didn't really fit in. She happened to have very short hair and wore pants.

"All of us usually wear pants," Tracy whispered, idly petting Fred.

"Shush," said Kaitlin. "It's probably an old story."

Plus, the fictional girl had one of those really neutral names, like "Pat" or "Dale." As Ms. Manon read the tale, it turned out that everyone at this new school thought the girl was actually a little boy.

"People used to think I was a boy when I was little," volunteered Winter. "I had really short hair."

"No one would think that now," said Chuck. Then he blushed profusely, right to the tips of his red hair.

Winter smiled, undisturbed. She turned around to whisper provocatively to Kaitlin. "It was a *formidable ordeal*." She emphasized the words purposefully.

When the girl in the story asked to visit the restroom, the fictional teacher made her go into the one marked "Boys," full of weird toilets called urinals.

"That happened to me when I was eight," Winter said ruefully. But then she added quickly, "Of course, I refused to go in!"

33

The boys were chortling at this point. Ms. Manon put down the book and gazed at her students. "Okay, boys," she inquired. "How many of you have ever been in a girls' washroom?" There was widespread laughter around the room. Then Glenn, leaning back nonchalantly in his chair, raised his hand. Chuck followed suit. Then nearly every other boy in the class raised his hand.

Kaitlin gazed about in wonder. Had they all looked into the girls' washroom, or were they just showing off?

Ms. Manon nodded as if it was what she'd suspected all along. "Now, girls," she said, "how many of you have ever been in the boys' washroom?"

No hands went up. Kaitlin looked at Tracy, who shook her head vigorously, but raised an eyebrow back at Kaitlin, who mouthed a big "No." Glenn poked lightly at Winter, who uttered an unequivocal "Don't look at me, man!"

Ms. Manon clapped her hands together. "All right, girls. We're going into the boys' washroom. Up, up, ladies, let's go."

A loud murmur ran through the class, as the girls uncertainly half-rose from their desks.

"I'm serious," said the teacher. "Come on. Boys, you stay here. Chuck, come along, please." Chuck protested, uncertain about why he was being included with the girls.

Kaitlin had to step over Glenn's running shoe because his outstretched leg nearly blocked the aisle.

"Need a tour guide, Kaitlin?" he asked.

"Keep it down, boys," Ms. Manon instructed. "We'll be right back."

With that, the girls and Chuck were all briskly

ushered out of the room. Kaitlin glanced back at the abandoned guys. Most were open-mouthed with a mixture of glee, disapproval and confusion.

The girls, for their part, were giggling nervously by the time they got to the big orange door. Ms. Manon sent Chuck in to make sure the coast was clear.

"It's an *outlandish* adventure," Kaitlin whispered, jabbing Winter. Her friend grinned and poked back.

Chuck returned after a moment, nodding to the teacher. "It's empty, Ms. Manon," he said, looking concerned.

"Thank you, Chuck," she said. "You may go back to class." Chuck wandered slowly, reluctantly down the hall, half-turning several times to look back at them.

Ms. Manon held the bathroom door open and waved the girls inward, but everyone hung back a bit. "For heavens' sakes," muttered Winter. She grabbed Kaitlin's arm, pulling her inside. The other girls followed.

At first glance, the sinks, walls and mirrors were similar to the parallel amenities in the girls' washroom, although adorned with slightly more graffiti. But there the similarities ended. All along one wall were strange, misshapen toilets, which Ms. Manon explained were urinals. Kaitlin had never seen one before, and she wasn't exactly sure how they were used. She felt slightly ill to her stomach, as if she was doing something wrong. Ms. Manon, as calm and collected as ever, pressed down on a handle, flushing it in demonstration. There were a few nervous giggles.

Ms. Manon smiled and nodded. "Okay, girls. We can go back to class."

Kaitlin wanted to run from the room, but she forced

herself to walk out at a normal pace. She could feel her heart beating loudly. Tracy's face looked rather white, and Ashley was now giggling non-stop with her hands pressed over her mouth. Only Winter appeared unconcerned.

Yet all the girls pulled themselves together before making their entrance back into class. Heads high, they walked back towards their desks and slid coolly into their seats. Ms. Manon gave them a subtle nod of approval.

The boys sank low in their seats. "Don't sulk, guys," Winter chided.

*   *   *

Kaitlin kicked at her books, trying unsuccessfully to get them to fit into the bottom of her locker. Exasperated, she grabbed two off the pile, managing to squish them onto the top shelf.

"Kaitlin Anderson, what a mess," teased Tracy, watching with amusement.

By contrast, Tracy's locker was perfectly organized, her binders arranged carefully by colours of the rainbow. Her gym shoes were tied together with a bow, hanging neatly on a hook. The entire inside surface of the locker was covered with glossy magazine photos of teen musicians and television idols. Tracy had even pasted a few of the young men inside Kaitlin's locker, mainly because Tracy had run out of room in her own locker, not out of idols.

Kaitlin had shrugged good-naturedly and allowed the invasion into her space. She'd stuck a bunch of bumper-stickers to the inside of the door. They had weird sayings written on them like: "If you can read this, you're too close," or "Beep if you're a Flames fan." Her all-time favourite was bright purple and read: "Have you hugged a cowboy today?"

Winter, for her part, had gone artistic, displaying intricate snowflakes cut out of coloured foil, and taped in overlapping patterns to the inside of her locker.

Ashley seemed to have her entire sticker collection pasted in hers, depicting everything from flowers and butterflies to monsters and skulls. There wasn't any apparent rhyme or reason to the images—the only prerequisite being an adhesive surface.

Kaitlin wasn't surprised that her group regularly got particularly hostile glares from the school janitor. She figured the poor fellow wasn't looking forward to scrubbing off all that stickiness at the end of the year.

She looked carefully at the latest addition to her own locker, courtesy of Tracy. A teenager in a tattered shirt gazed back at her with a wide gleaming grin. But she could only see one blue eye; unevenly cut hair spilled over half his face. "Is this guy partly deformed or something?" Kaitlin asked blandly.

"What!" exclaimed Tracy. "Of course not! What do you mean?" She peered closely at the photo herself.

"Why is his face half-covered?" Kaitlin queried. "I think there must be something wrong with him."

"Wrong with him?" Tracy echoed. "He's perfect!" She poked at Kaitlin. "That's just his hairstyle, silly."

"I say he's hiding something."

Winter chortled, the sound muffled within the walls of her locker as she bent to arrange her own books.

Tracy glowered at them both. Then she coughed warningly as a large group of Grade Eight boys sauntered towards them. Even Winter straightened up, looking wary.

"Hi there, Kaitlin," Michael drawled, emphasizing her name so much it was almost three syllables. He put a hand against the door of her locker, holding it open. He briefly eyed the poster Tracy had pasted there. His friends, mainly from the basketball team, carried their gym-bags over their shoulders like badges of honour. They glanced curiously at the girls but didn't say anything. Michael's best friend Brad stood beside him, nearly as tall as Michael. When they were younger, Brad, Michael and Kaitlin used to toss around a basketball in Michael's driveway. Kaitlin wondered if Brad remembered that.

Kaitlin scowled at Michael, trying to ignore his friends, not an easy thing to do. All the other Grade Seven girls were gaping openly. The Grade Eight guys didn't usually hang out much with seventh graders, and vice versa. Now, as the boys loomed in the small hallway, Kaitlin noticed they seemed a fair bit bigger than most of her classmates, except maybe Glenn.

"Go away," she said, staring balefully at Michael. She pulled suddenly at the door to her locker, releasing it from his loose hold. Pushing it closed, she frowned into that familiar hated face.

A few of the guys laughed, enjoying the put-down. Tracy poked Kaitlin in the ribs in rebuke, but Kaitlin tried to ignore her.

Michael only grinned. "Hello, Tracy."

"Hi, Michael," she answered in her sweetest voice, the one that Kaitlin particularly hated.

"And Ashley, Winter," Michael added courteously. Ashley stammered something unintelligible. Winter raised an eyebrow and returned a curt nod.

"So, Kaitlin," he said, "we hear that you girls had an unusual field trip today." Kaitlin stared back at him fiercely. He continued: "Did you learn anything?"

The other guys burst out laughing. Michael swung his own gym bag over his shoulder. "School is such an educational institution, isn't it?" He winked at Tracy, and the group sauntered off.

Brad called out over his shoulder, "Just let us know if you need another tour, girls." The guys laughed again, although Michael only smiled.

"Boys are pigs," Kaitlin growled.

"*Delinquents*," said Winter archly.

"*Reprobates*," Kaitlin countered. Winter nodded with a smile, conceding the round.

Ashley and Tracy looked at them blankly.

"I kind of like Michael," Tracy mumbled. "Hey, Kaitlin," she added suddenly, "I was wondering if we could hang out after school."

"Yeah, I think that would be cool. Should we go to your place?"

"Well," Tracy answered slowly, "I thought it would be more fun at your house, if that's okay." Her voice sounded a bit funny. Kaitlin eyed her closely for a moment, then shrugged it off.

"Let me hold Fred for a while, though," said Kaitlin, making a big show as they walked of petting the little dog. She stiffened as she saw Michael leaning over his own locker down the hall. Shelley Whitfield was standing very close beside him, hanging on to his elbow.

Kaitlin took a deep breath. She resolved to fend off any more conversational attempts by totally ignoring Michael when he spoke to her.

But as the girls passed by, Michael was smiling at the giggling Shelley. He didn't seem to notice them at all.

*   *   *

The rain had finally let up. A small break in the clouds showed a crack of deep blue sky. Kaitlin squinted at it, unimpressed. She carefully fitted her key into the lock, waiting for the familiar click.

She tossed her straw hat into the closet, pausing to lock the door behind them.

It would only be an hour or so before Jane came home from work, after picking up Anna from daycare. Kaitlin rather liked having the whole house to herself, but she didn't mind sharing the time with her best friend Tracy either.

"Do you want a snack?" she asked as they dumped their backpacks onto the kitchen table. The room was bright with lots of windows. Kaitlin's dad had done a major renovation on that part of the house just the year before. Dried fruit and garlic hung on a string off one corner of the cupboard, but that was just a decoration.

"Sure. What do you have?"

Kaitlin opened the refrigerator, leaning inside. "There's a bunch of fruit: apples, pears and plums. And there are some cinnamon rolls. That's what I'm going to have."

"Me too," said Tracy promptly.

Both girls carefully unrolled the pastry, breaking off pieces as they went. "Jane's a good cook," said Tracy.

Kaitlin shrugged. "My dad made these."

"Really?" asked Tracy, looking surprised.

"Yeah," said Kaitlin. "I think Anna might have helped, though." That thought forced them both to eye the remainder of their rolls suspiciously for a moment. "My dad's a decent chef. Better than Jane. But he gets home from work later at night, so usually Jane cooks. Or sometimes I make spaghetti."

"You know how to cook?" Tracy seemed impressed.

"Well…not much," Kaitlin admitted. "I make spaghetti and pancakes, and that's about it."

"Maybe I should cook too," Tracy mused, licking the cinnamon off a piece of her roll.

"Sure, whatever. If you're looking for recipes, you should ask Winter, she cooks like crazy. When I went over there, she made a soufflé for dinner and strawberry sorbet for dessert. For her whole family— six people, plus me. That's insane, I think."

"Winter's kind of a show-off."

"That's why I like her."

Tracy stuck her tongue out at Kaitlin. They were both laughing when Jane's car pulled up in the driveway.

Anna ran into the house. "Is Mrs. Telgord back yet?" she asked eagerly.

"What?" Tracy asked, choking a bit on the last of her roll. She swivelled in her chair to look at Kaitlin, as if she hadn't heard quite right.

"Mrs. Telgord went to heaven," Anna told Tracy.

"Yes, I heard. I'm sorry."

Anna turned her wide blue gaze up to Tracy. "Don't worry. She'll be back soon. To bake me brownies."

Kaitlin shook her head. "My half-sister has mental problems."

Jane gave Kaitlin a stern look as she dumped an armful of groceries onto the counter. "You know that's not true, Kaitlin. She's just too young to understand properly." She turned her attention to Tracy. "Hi, Tracy, how are you?"

"I'm fine, Jane," said Tracy, using that annoying voice again. "How are you?"

Jane smiled. "I'm fine too, thank you." She bent down on her knees, close to Anna. "Sweetie, Mrs. Telgord is in heaven. She can't come back here, because she lives in heaven now."

Anna's big eyes filled slowly with tears. She shook her head. "No, she's making brownies," the girl insisted. "She promised."

Jane stroked Anna's curls and kissed her forehead, but Anna refused to be comforted. She broke away and ran into the other room, sniffling. Tracy and Kaitlin watched a bit awkwardly. "Poor kid," said Tracy, staring after her.

Tracy didn't have any sisters or brothers, so she couldn't possibly understand how much of a pest Anna was, Kaitlin thought.

"I guess," she said dryly, pouring glasses of milk for herself and Tracy. She took the chocolate milk powder out of the cupboard, and both girls dropped in several tablespoons of chocolate, stirring vigorously.

"Don't spoil your dinner, Kaitlin," advised Jane.

Kaitlin rolled her eyes and kept stirring. There's nothing worse than lumpy chocolate milk.

Jane briskly unpacked the groceries, storing milk, fruit, cereal and cookies in the refrigerator and cupboards.

The doorbell rang loudly, startling everyone.

"Will you get that, Kaitlin?" Jane asked from her perch on the stool, hiding extra candies on the very top shelf that only Kaitlin's father could easily reach. Kaitlin didn't much care for those plain white mints, but Anna liked them. Kaitlin figured it was the "what-Anna-can't-reach-won't-hurt-her" philosophy.

Grumbling, Kaitlin headed for the door. An earnest-looking young man stood there smiling, holding a clipboard. Kaitlin scrunched up her face doubtfully, staring at him.

"Hello, miss," he said, brightly cheerful.

Kaitlin scowled.

"Is your mother home?" he asked, still smiling.

Kaitlin arranged her face in its most bland expression. "My mother is dead," she said, staring straight at him.

He blanched. "Oh, my goodness, I'm so sorry. I…" he stammered, losing his lines. Beads of sweat appeared on his forehead.

"May I help you?" asked Jane in clipped tones, stepping up to the door. She didn't look at Kaitlin, but her expression was grim.

Kaitlin scrambled back into the kitchen as Jane carefully explained that she had already given to the man's charity recently. Kaitlin saw him walk back towards the road.

She glanced at the clock. "Isn't your father picking you up at five?" she hissed quietly at Tracy.

Tracy nodded, sipping at her milk.

"Let's wait outside," she whispered, poking Tracy as her friend took big gulps of her drink, trying to finish it quickly. But Jane stood in the doorway to the kitchen. She had a funny look on her face.

Kaitlin took a deep breath. "We're going to wait outside for Tracy's Dad," she said, lifting her chin a little, waiting for Jane to meet her gaze.

But Jane just stepped aside. "Goodnight, Tracy." She picked up the empty glasses and put them in the dishwasher.

"Thank you, Jane," said Tracy politely. "Goodnight."

The air in the kitchen felt very thick. Kaitlin had a strange, unpleasant feeling in the pit of her stomach. She grabbed Tracy's wrist. "Come on," she said, opening the front door and pulling her friend outside.

They almost fell over Anna, who was sitting on the step, staring mournfully at Mrs. Telgord's little white house with the yellow curtains.

*　　*　　*

Dinner was a quiet affair, despite Anna's incessant chatter about the boy at daycare who'd got stuck in the monkey-bars and the firefighters who had come to free him. Ever since then, the other kids had been unsuccessfully trying to get themselves stuck too.

The tuna casserole Jane had made was dry, but Kaitlin tried to force herself to eat it. It seemed the wisest course of action.

Anna didn't seem to agree. "I don't like it, Mommy," she protested, pushing the food around her plate in a futile attempt to minimize it.

Jane sighed deeply. "How about you, Kaitlin? Do you like it?" she asked pointedly.

Kaitlin stared at the food, uncertain of how to answer. "Well…"

"I don't like it," said Jane suddenly. She jumped up, grabbing Anna's and Kaitlin's plates as well as her own and aggressively dumping the food into the garbage. Kaitlin's father hung tightly onto his when it looked like Jane would take that too. "Wait," he protested. "I love it." He munched on it, pasting a particularly happy expression on his face. Jane frowned angrily at him.

She pulled a bunch of containers out of the cupboard and fridge, letting everything bang a little more than might have been necessary. She started making a peanut butter sandwich for Anna. "Do you want one, Kaitlin?" Jane asked tonelessly.

"No," said Kaitlin uneasily. "No, thank you." She sipped cautiously at her milk.

After Kaitlin and her dad had cleared up the table, he asked her for help in the garage. "I'm finishing off that cabinet for your room," he said.

Kaitlin nodded. "Sure. Will you make it match my bed?"

"Of course. I know I'd be in big trouble if I didn't."

Kaitlin grinned at him, and he ruffled her hair as they

headed towards the garage. "I want to help too, Daddy," Anna said eagerly, her eyes wide and hopeful.

He picked up the little girl, tossing her into the air while she giggled and shrieked in delight. He kissed her forehead and set her down carefully. "I'll make something with just you in a while, but right now I'm going to make something with Kaitlin."

Anna's lip trembled as if she hadn't quite made up her mind whether to cry or not. "Will you do me a favour, sweetie?" he asked. "Will you keep your Mommy company while I'm working?" He tickled her cheek.

She nodded, giggling. "Okay, Daddy."

"Good girl," he said as she ran off to find Jane.

In the garage, Kaitlin worked silently with her dad, carefully sanding the edges of her cabinet. They started with quite coarse sandpaper and eventually progressed to very fine paper that felt almost rubbery against Kaitlin's palm.

"So, Kaitlin," said her dad finally.

"Uh-huh…" responded Kaitlin, intent on her work.

"I wish you'd be nice to Jane," he said, sanding carefully around a corner.

"I thought you said you wanted me to be polite to Jane."

"Hmm," said her father quietly. "Let's just say I'm now asking you to go one step further and actually be nice."

Kaitlin felt a sinking feeling in her chest, and her heart was beating a bit faster than felt comfortable. "I don't like her, Dad," she said, very softly.

He put down his sandpaper and leaned back on his heels, giving her his full attention. "Why, Katie? Tell me why you don't like her."

Kaitlin didn't answer, her mind working rapidly, searching for an explanation.

"Doesn't she treat you well?"

Kaitlin shrugged. She felt tense, and her mouth was dry. "I guess so."

Her father continued to watch her with an unreadable look in his eyes.

"I don't think she likes me."

Her father moved beside her on the step and wrapped his arm closely around her. "I think she does," he whispered. "But more than that, I know she loves you."

Kaitlin opened her mouth to protest, but he put a finger lightly against her bottom lip. "Sweetheart, you've been an absolutely critical part of Jane's life these past six years. Let me tell you some stuff." He leaned back on the step. "Jane learned to sew, just so she could make you the outlandish Halloween costumes you always demanded. I couldn't believe it. Did you know Jane would cry every time we had to take you for a vaccination, even when it didn't really bother you? And if you're ever the slightest bit late getting home from your friends' houses, she paces the floor and watches the window. Did you know that?" he asked, nudging her slightly.

Kaitlin shook her head.

"When Jane and I got married, she wasn't just marrying me; she was marrying into our family, marrying both of us, really," he said earnestly. "I would never lie to you. I want you to believe that Jane loves you." He sounded very serious.

Taking a deep breath, she whispered, "I want my real mother, though."

She could feel him stiffen beside her. He sighed, then relaxed slightly. "I know, baby. As long as I live, I'll miss your mother. I loved her so much. You know that." He lightly caressed her hair. "I will always love her. I'll never forget the wonder of your mother." He paused, staring down at his big hands. "But...but the pain is going away. Because I have you and Jane and Anna to make living worthwhile." He fell silent beside her.

Kaitlin wrapped her arms around him and pressed her face against his warm chest. Her tears dampened his shirt.

"Will you think about what I've said, Katie?" he asked, very quietly stroking her hair. "Just think about it, please?"

She nodded mutely.

Her father gave her a soft hug. Then, keeping an arm around her, he picked up a piece of the fine sandpaper and lightly sanded the wood.

Five

The wind blew softly, rustling the dry grass at Kaitlin's feet. She sat on a large tree root at the edge of the schoolyard, gazing about at the brightly coloured T-shirts, runners and backpacks. She was supposed to be waiting for Tracy, who was writing a make-up English test after missing a day of school the week before. Kaitlin had glanced about for Winter or Ashley, but not spying either immediately, she'd opted for solitude.

She pushed the toe of her shoe in the dirt, idly drawing vaguely symmetrical patterns in the sand.

A light tap on the back of her hat nearly knocked it off her head. Kaitlin jumped, startled. Holding onto the hat, she turned quickly, disconcerted to see Glenn standing there, grinning at her. "Hey, Kaitlin," he said. "So what's with the hat?"

She blinked at him, resetting it properly on her head with an extra little tug to make it more resistant to boy tampering. "Hi, Glenn." She felt vaguely alarmed to find him in her space.

He looked downwards towards the ground, as if searching for a seat. For a moment, Kaitlin considered moving over to make room for him on her root, but dismissed the idea. It wasn't like she was inviting his company or anything.

But Glenn settled down on another root, more or less facing her. He had a quizzical expression on his face.

"What?" she asked. "Oh. You don't like my hat?" Then, before he could answer, she lifted her chin defiantly. "I like it," she said.

"Sure, it's fine. Just different is all."

"Oh," said Kaitlin, thinking quickly. "Well, of course it is. I'm unique."

Glenn laughed. "Hey, I won't argue with you there."

"The hat certainly seems to have got *your* attention," she said pointedly.

"Ah. It might not be the hat."

Kaitlin could feel her face going warm. She wondered if he were making fun of her. "I think it's the hat," she countered.

Before she knew what was happening, he reached across and lifted the hat in question clear off her head. He laid it down beside him and grinned shamelessly at her. Kaitlin smoothed her hair nervously. "No, it's definitely not the hat," he said.

Kaitlin's face felt very hot, and she wasn't sure where to look. A change of topic seemed to be in order. "So, do you like it here?" she asked lamely.

"Here?" Glenn gave her a curious look, glancing about. "It's quite a fine tree, sure," he said.

"No!" exclaimed Kaitlin. "I meant, since you moved here. Do you like it okay?"

"Ah," said Glenn. "Hmm." He seemed to be thinking

the matter over. "It's pretty quiet, don't you think? The uh…neighbourhood?" He drew out the last word almost mockingly. "But that keeps me out of trouble, my mother says."

She squinted at him.

"I miss my dad," he admitted candidly. "I only see him once a week."

Kaitlin nodded. "I miss my mom."

"Oh?" asked Glenn, interested. "Your folks split up?"

"No," said Kaitlin. "She's dead."

"Sheesh," said Glenn awkwardly, "I'm sorry. That must be rough. How old were you when she died?"

"Five," Kaitlin answered softly. "I worry about not remembering her enough, but I do remember her."

Glenn nodded. "Sure. I remember stuff from when I was four, maybe even three. What do you remember most?"

Kaitlin paused, surprised that he'd ask that sort of question. She pondered silently for a moment, then: "I remember going for walks, holding my mom's hand. I remember sitting in her lap while she read me a story. I remember her making pigtails in my hair and laughing when she messed up the braiding. I remember when she was so sick in the hospital and she was too weak to really hug me…"

She shrugged, and her voice trailed off. She looked up to see Glenn watching her intently. "I can't even imagine that. That's really awful," he said quietly.

"My dad got remarried."

"And is she one of those wicked stepmothers who locks you in the basement and feeds you dry bread?"

His gaze roamed over her designer clothes and settled on her fancy lunch containers.

"She hasn't done that yet," Kaitlin muttered.

"Maybe I'm wrong, but I think in a divorce, it's got to be just a little bit like having a parent die—especially when you don't see them," said Glenn. "My mom didn't let me see my dad for about three months when they first split. And everyone told me off if I complained. I could have used some sympathy, I think." But then he shrugged as if he didn't really care.

"Yeah, that sucks too," Kaitlin said.

He smiled suddenly. "It does, doesn't it?" He glanced at his watch. "Hey! I was supposed to be at basketball practice about five minutes ago. You made me late," he said.

She didn't say anything.

He got up, brushing off his jeans. He picked up her straw hat and carefully set it back on her head, then he paused for a moment. "See you, Kaitlin," he said as he finally strolled off.

"Bye, Glenn," she said quietly. Then she glanced down, looking at the shapes she'd been drawing in the sand. Absently, she obliterated one of them with her toe.

"Oh, here you are!" exclaimed Tracy, walking up with Winter. "I've been looking everywhere for you!"

"She was talking to a *boy*," drawled Winter, her voice low and teasing right behind Kaitlin's ear. Kaitlin turned furiously, scowling at Winter, then back at Tracy.

"Shut up, all of you," said Kaitlin, pulling the brim of her hat down over her eyes.

On Tuesdays and Thursdays, Kaitlin and her friends carried bag lunches to school, but the decent cafeteria chef worked on Monday, Wednesday and Friday, so on those days they bought lunch.

Kaitlin frowned as she watched Michael and Shelley walk by her table in the cafeteria. They were carrying their food trays, deep in conversation.

Almost without thinking about it, she stuck out her foot. Michael stumbled. His tray wavered precariously, and his glass of milk fell to the floor with an impressive crash. Liquid splattered everywhere.

Shelley shrieked in dismay.

Immediately, the cafeteria broke out into cheers and applause. Michael smoothly set down the remainder of his tray and lifted his arms into the air, good-naturedly accepting the laughter.

When the noise had settled down, he walked back over to Kaitlin and stared down at her. Her heart beat very fast, and she glared back at him defiantly. "No use crying over spilt milk," she gasped.

With his smile fixed on his face, Michael leaned very close to her ear. "For your sake, I'm going to assume that was an accident." He straightened and rejoined Shelley.

Winter raised an eyebrow. "That splashed on my boots. I hope it was worth it."

Kaitlin scowled.

*   *   *

"Do you want to hang out after school?" Tracy asked, prodding Kaitlin lightly.

"Ouch. Okay. Let's go to your place."

"Well, it's more fun at your house."

"Tracy, I haven't been to your place in months. I need a break from Anna and her morbid brownie obsession. If it's okay with your parents, I want to visit you."

Tracy nodded slowly. "Sure," she said, but her face looked pinched as she carefully piled her books into her backpack.

"Oh, just one second, I'd better leave a voice message for Jane," said Kaitlin. After her conversation with her father about Jane's pacing and looking out of windows, she supposed she ought to at least let Jane know she'd be home late. She left a quick voice mail message, including Tracy's phone number. She dialled the number to Jane's office to leave a message with Jane's assistant as well.

"Your place is where'd she call first anyhow, if she was looking for me," Kaitlin grumbled more to herself than to Tracy, as they left the school.

"Oh, I know," Tracy answered. "My dad would call your place too, if he couldn't find me."

"Wouldn't your mom as well?"

"What?" said Tracy. "Yes, of course, Mom and Dad both know you're my best friend."

Kaitlin smiled, pleased.

Tracy's house was about six blocks away from school. The girls hefted their knapsacks onto their backs and walked along, chatting. Kaitlin supposed she had just imagined Tracy's reluctance to invite her over. But once inside the door, Kaitlin thought she understood the problem. The place was a mess; she couldn't believe it. Newspapers, dirty dishes and leftover food were scattered all over the living room and the kitchen. Tracy didn't offer Kaitlin a snack. Instead, the girls went right up to Tracy's room.

Unlike Kaitlin's typically messy bedroom, Tracy's domain was usually spotless. But not now. The room looked like it hadn't been vacuumed in weeks. It was in nearly as much disarray as the rest of the house. Tracy, who typically hung up every piece of clothing the moment she took it off, had shirts and socks scattered all over the floor of her bedroom. The bed wasn't even made.

Kaitlin shivered.

For a moment she wondered if an alien had taken over her friend's body. Tracy's bedroom was usually pretty and tidy, and best of all, it had a washroom of its own. Kaitlin didn't say anything about the state of the house. She felt sorry for insisting on coming over.

Tracy tugged up her bedspread so the two girls could sprawl across the lumpy surface, then she pulled out a bunch of magazines, mainly to ogle the teenage musicians and movie stars inside. Kaitlin turned the pages unenthusiastically.

"I just love these tans," gushed Tracy, displaying a photo of California surfers. "When I get a boyfriend, he's going to have to be tanned like this."

Kaitlin rolled her eyes. "These boys are definitely going to get skin cancer," she said, tapping the page.

Tracy threw a pillow at Kaitlin.

When the phone rang, they had to scramble to find it,

as it was buried under a pile of clothes. "Hello?" Tracy answered breathlessly. "Oh, Jane," she said, smiling.

Kaitlin made a face.

"Yes, she's right here." Tracy handed the phone over to Kaitlin.

Kaitlin stuck her tongue out at Tracy as she took the phone. "Sure. Okay. Bye."

Afterwards, she pushed the phone back into its place under the clothes pile. She shrugged at Tracy. "Jane's going to swing by here to pick me up. She just got Anna from daycare. I'm going to wait outside."

Tracy nodded. "Okay. I'll walk you out then."

Kaitlin tried not to step on any clothes or paper as she made her way downstairs. But because she was watching her feet so carefully, she almost didn't notice Tracy's father. They narrowly avoided colliding in the hallway.

"Kaitlin!" he exclaimed jovially. Mr. Leeland was carrying a dark bottle. Kaitlin wondered if it was beer. She watched as the liquid swirled about the open bottle every time Tracy's father gestured. "You haven't been around for the longest time, dear," he said, waving his arm.

Kaitlin eyed him. His face was red, and his eyes looked weird. But he smiled at the girls. "Sorry about the mess, Kaitlin. We just need to get more organized…" His voice trailed off.

Tracy linked her arm through Kaitlin's, pulling her along insistently towards the door. But Mr. Leeland followed doggedly. "Kaitlin, dear, I want to thank you," he insisted.

Kaitlin paused, ignoring Tracy's pulling. "What for?" she asked.

"For being such a marvellously good friend to Tracy," he said, with a flourish. "It's been hard on us both, since her mother left." He waved again and turned back into the house.

Tracy's eyes were filling with tears, and her lip was quivering.

"Your Mom left?" Kaitlin asked, astonished.

Tracy didn't answer.

Just then, Jane's car pulled into the driveway. "Hi!" Anna yelled, leaning out of the window, waving frantically.

Kaitlin could feel her heart beating fast in confusion. It looked like Jane and Anna were about to get out of the car, and Tracy looked liked she was about to break down crying.

Finally, Kaitlin said, very firmly, "I'll talk to you tomorrow, Tracy."

Tracy nodded and ran back into her house. Kaitlin stared after her for a moment, then slid into Jane's car. "Let's just go," she said.

She slumped against the seat, feeling scared for Tracy, but also confused and hurt. Why hadn't her best friend told her that her mother had left? She sighed deeply, frowning out her window.

From the driver's seat, Jane glanced in her rear-view mirror at Kaitlin, then back at the door to Tracy's house. She started the car. Then, glancing again at Kaitlin, she asked tentatively: "Is everything okay with you and Tracy? Your goodbye looked a little...off. And don't forget to buckle your seatbelt, please," she added.

"Why wouldn't Tracy have told me her mother

doesn't live there any more?" Kaitlin asked, not really expecting an answer. In her distress, she'd forgotten her rule about avoiding all possible conversation with Jane. She frowned at Anna in the front seat, who was happily singing a daycare song about a butterfly.

"Tracy's mom left?" Jane repeated slowly. "How sad for Tracy. She just told you now?"

"No!" Kaitlin exclaimed. "Her father told me. Tracy didn't even tell me herself."

Jane sighed. "Tracy must be feeling very bad right now, dear. You're going to have to be extra-nice to her for a while, I think."

"Hey," Kaitlin protested indignantly. "I'm always extra-nice to Tracy. She's my best friend."

Jane smiled. "It's a very good thing to have a best friend, Kaitlin. But she's going to need your support now."

"She doesn't act like it," Kaitlin mumbled.

Jane opened her mouth as if she were going to say more, but she was drowned out by a particularly loud butterfly chorus. "Sing!" Anna shrieked, waving her arms in the air. "Everybody sing!"

Jane gave Kaitlin a helpless look in the mirror. But she dutifully hummed along to the song about the butterfly as she drove.

*　　*　　*

Kaitlin waited at Tracy's locker the next morning before school, but her friend hadn't arrived by the time the bell rang. Tracy slipped into class a few minutes late, mumbling an apology to the teacher. "Don't make a habit of it, Tracy," Ms. Manon advised.

Then, at lunch, Tracy dashed out the classroom door the moment the bell rang. Ms. Manon hadn't even finished the history homework instructions. Kaitlin grabbed her books and hurried after her friend. Tracy was almost out of the school before Kaitlin caught up. "Are you running away from me?" Kaitlin protested, tugging on Tracy's backpack.

"I'm just busy. I've got to hurry." She pushed through the door, as if in a rush.

Kaitlin felt hurt, but she took a very deep breath and followed her friend. "Tracy," she said, laying her hand very gently on the girl's arm, "I'm sorry your mom left. You know you're my best friend, and if you want to talk about it, I'm here."

For a moment, Kaitlin thought Tracy was going to yell or hit her; she had such an anguished look on her face. But then her eyes filled with tears. "She doesn't love my dad any more," Tracy whispered. "They fought some, but I didn't know she was going to leave. There was a note waiting for me one day when I got home." Then Tracy started crying, right in the middle of the schoolyard.

Kaitlin led her away from the busy doorway, and they leaned against the school wall. There was an awful squeezing in Kaitlin's stomach. She didn't know what to say. Her own mother hadn't wanted to leave her family. She couldn't even imagine Jane ever doing something like that.

Tracy didn't need any more prompting. She dropped her backpack and covered her face with her hands, crying bitterly. "She's got a new place across town. Why can't she stay with my dad and me?

"My dad is so sad. He cries all the time, when he thinks I can't hear." The tears were pouring down Tracy's face now, and between sobs, she was gasping for breath. Kaitlin was crying too. She had no idea what to say, but she wrapped her arms tightly around her friend and held her.

After several minutes, Tracy pulled back, trying to wipe away her tears. She glanced worriedly about the schoolyard. "People are looking at me," she hiccuped.

"No, no, they're not," Kaitlin soothed, trying to comfort her friend.

"Yes, yes, they are!" Tracy insisted, her voice becoming hysterical.

Kaitlin looked around. Several students were noticeably gaping at them. "You just never mind," she said firmly. "Let's go find a bathroom so you can wash your face. That will make you feel better."

Aaargh, she thought. *I sound like Jane!* She dismissed the thought with a confused shake of her head. She picked up Tracy's backpack and carried it as they pushed through the crowd. Tracy kept her head down, rushing into the school.

Chuck moved uncertainly in front of them, but Kaitlin intervened. "Go away," she hissed unceremoniously at him. Chuck coloured and fell back.

Once inside, Tracy dashed for the sanctuary of the washroom. Kaitlin followed, grasping Tracy's backpack tightly against her chest.

Suddenly, Michael stepped into Kaitlin's path. His

face was perfectly serious for once. He glanced quickly at Tracy's fleeing back. Then he stared into Kaitlin's own wet eyes. "Is everything okay, Kaitlin?"

She lifted her chin to meet his gaze firmly. "No," she said, "nothing at all is okay." She stepped around Michael and followed her friend.

Six

In the mirror, Katerina was looking far too prim and proper, with her hair all combed flat and pulled back demurely by a wide purple ribbon. Kaitlin stuck out her tongue and Katerina, not surprisingly, immediately returned the gesture.

There was a frantic pounding on her bedroom door, the unmistakable sound of four-year-old fists hammering impatiently. "Kaitlin, Kaitlin, let me in! I want to come IN!" Anna pleaded loudly. The little girl wailed piteously for a few seconds, then resumed pounding. "Kaitlin, open the door! I want in!"

Kaitlin smiled, ignoring the request. The new lock on the door had done wonders for her disposition. She could hear the little feet kicking against the wood of the door. After waiting what seemed like an appropriate length of time to get her half-sister into a full frenzy, Kaitlin smoothly slid the lock and pulled the door open.

Anna stumbled inside.

"So what do you want?" Kaitlin eyed the red-faced little girl, all dolled up in her best Sunday ribbons and lace.

"I want to come in."

"That's what I thought."

Anna peered with interest about the room. She tried the door to Kaitlin's new cabinet. "It's locked," she exclaimed.

"I know," Kaitlin nodded sagely.

"What's in it?" Anna asked, tugging on the door.

"Very fun things," Kaitlin grinned, baiting her. "Candies and cookies and all kinds of cool toys."

Anna was wide-eyed, staring at the lock. "Really?" she asked.

"Maybe," Kaitlin responded coyly. "Could be."

Anna looked uncertainly at Kaitlin, her gaze coming finally to rest at Kaitlin's feet. "Your shoes are wrong," Anna pointed out.

Kaitlin couldn't help laughing. "I know." She sat on the edge of her bed, staring down at her feet. The right foot was bare and clad in a sandal. The left was adorned in an ankle sock and a shiny thick-soled black shoe. She swung her legs, contemplating each, trying to decide which would go best with her purple top and skirt.

Jane leaned against the doorframe. "Are you girls almost ready? We'll be leaving in a few minutes." Jane eyed Kaitlin's feet. "The sandals look quite nice, Kaitlin. That's what I'd go with." She held her hand out to Anna. "Come here, sweets. I want to rebrush your hair. You've messed it up again."

"Yes, Mommy." Anna allowed herself to be led out of the room. "Kaitlin has candies and cookies and toys locked up in her room?" Anna asked plaintively, her voice disappearing as they moved down the hall.

Kaitlin glanced in the mirror again, seeing Katerina's

rebuking glance. "Oh, I know," she replied crossly. "I won't take Jane's advice." She quickly took off the sandal and pulled on the other sock and black shoe.

*   *   *

The worst thing about Sunday School, Kaitlin thought, was Michael Drayson. Because the Grade Seven and Grade Eight kids were in the same class, once a week Kaitlin was forced to sit in the same room as her arch-enemy. She fixed a stern expression on her face as she peeked into her Sunday School room. Most of the kids were already seated, but there was no sign of Michael. *Perhaps they're away for the weekend*, Kaitlin thought. *Maybe he's sick.* She smiled warmly at that idea. *Maybe he's moved away.* Her mind raced with the delicious possibilities.

"What doesn't kill you makes you stronger," a deep voice whispered in her ear. She scowled and stormed into the room, throwing herself into a chair.

Michael strolled slowly behind her. "So," he said loudly, to the room. "Is that seat beside you available, Kaitlin?"

"Don't even think about it," she hissed, glaring up at him. All the Sunday School kids were staring at her. Kaitlin didn't care. She would have kicked the chair in question away from her to settle the matter, but it was wedged between her own chair and the next kid's. She struggled with it to push it away.

"Oh, here," Michael said smoothly. "Don't trouble yourself. I can get that." He lifted the chair a little, unhooking it from the next one, and slid in beside Kaitlin, just as Reverend Brown, who taught the junior-high class, stepped into the room and pulled the door closed behind him. Kaitlin was forced to stifle an angry comment.

Reverend. Brown took attendance and told the class the day's lesson would be on the Good Samaritan.

Kaitlin stared at the table as the minister went over the familiar details. She glanced discreetly sideways at Michael, who appeared to be listening intently to the story. Basically, it was about a guy who'd been beaten up by robbers. A priest went by, saw him and crossed on the other side of the street. Then a Levite, which was another really religious guy, came along. He also passed by on the other side of the street. But then came the Samaritan. When the Samaritan saw the injured man, he bandaged him up. Then he put him on his own donkey and took him to be helped.

"So which of these was really a good neighbour?" Reverend Brown asked. A thin girl waved her hand eagerly.

"Yes, Molly?" the minister prompted.

"The Samaritan was the good neighbour," the girl responded happily.

Reverend Brown nodded. "So when the Bible says to love your neighbour as yourself, does that just mean your real neighbour?"

The kids shook their heads solemnly.

"So who is your neighbour?"

"People who need help," said Molly.

"Kids in Africa," volunteered a boy.

"Sick people in hospitals!" someone else shouted.

"Terrorists!" yet another kid added. They were really getting into it now.

"Excuse me, Reverend Brown," Michael interrupted, leaning forward earnestly. "But your neighbour could literally mean your actual real next-door neighbour too, right?"

Kaitlin gasped in pure outrage.

The minister blinked. "Oh, yes, well, of course. You should love your real neighbours too."

Kaitlin kicked Michael hard under the table. He grunted softly but continued: "But what if my neighbour is mean and very difficult to love? Do I still have to?"

Reverend Brown nodded. "Thanks for bringing that point up, Michael. We can't just be willing to love our friends. We need to be willing to love those people who are particularly difficult to like."

Some of the other kids were grinning, their glances darting towards Kaitlin. She could feel her face burning as the minister dismissed the class.

"Thank you for raising those interesting points, Michael," he said approvingly as the kids streamed out of the class. "You were particularly quiet today, Kaitlin. Is everything okay?"

"Fine, sir, just fine," mumbled Kaitlin, slipping out of the room. For once, she sought Michael out. She pushed him in the back. He turned around with a surprised look on his face. "Why, Kaitlin, hello," he said, with an annoyingly big smile.

Kaitlin lifted her head defiantly. She leaned very close and whispered fiercely: "You, Michael Drayson, are going to be very, very sorry."

"Yes, Kaitlin," he said with false meekness. "I'm sure you're right."

She tossed her hair angrily over her shoulder, turned on her heel and strode away from the odious boy.

Seven

Gramma is coming, Gramma is coming!" an enthusiastic Anna proclaimed, hopping about the kitchen. She reached behind her to hold one foot in the air as she jumped up and down. Every now and then, the little girl would completely lose her balance and tumble to the floor, but she didn't seem to mind.

Kaitlin squinted at the formidable energy. "She's not your Gramma, Anna," she said. "She's just mine."

Anna paused, disconcerted. "Mommy!" she yelled loudly.

Jane, who was standing just a few feet away peeling potatoes, blinked. "Yes, Anna?" she asked.

"Is Gramma MINE?" the four-year-old implored.

Jane glanced over at Kaitlin for a moment before turning back to Anna. "Well, honey, Gramma is Kaitlin's grandmother. But she doesn't mind at all if you call her Gramma."

"Why does Kaitlin get her own grandmother?" Anna asked, perplexed.

"Gramma was Kaitlin's mommy's mommy, Anna. I think you know that," Jane explained.

"Kaitlin's mommy is in heaven, right?"

"That's right."

"With Mrs. Telgord?"

Jane nodded. "Yes, they're both in heaven, Anna."

Kaitlin watched her sister warily, wondering if the brownies were going to come back into the discussion. But Anna had other things on her mind. She scrunched up her face, her gaze flitting between Kaitlin and Jane. Finally she turned back to Jane. "But will Gramma bring me a surprise?" she asked, coming to the crux of the matter.

Jane burst out laughing. Even Kaitlin couldn't help smiling, but she covered it quickly with a scowl.

"I can't promise that, sweetie, but she usually does," said Jane.

Anna was satisfied. She grabbed hold of her shoe and resumed her jumping. "Gramma is coming! Gramma is coming!" she chanted.

Kaitlin finished chopping some green peppers and carried them out to her dad on the back patio, who was partly obscured by a cloud of smoke as he bent over the barbecue.

"Hi, Katie!" he exclaimed, before the smoke overcame him, and he started coughing.

Kaitlin eyed him doubtfully. He hadn't actually started cooking anything yet and was already streaked with soot. "Do you know what you're doing, Dad?" she asked.

"What?" he asked in an injured tone. "Of course! It's under control."

"Uh-huh," said Kaitlin as she reached up to wipe a streak of ash off her father's cheek.

"No, really," he protested. "Look. It's going fine now."

Kaitlin glanced at the barbecue. Indeed, the smoke

had died down somewhat. She handed him the dish of peppers.

"Thank you, sweetie," he said as he fiddled with the knobs on the barbecue a bit more.

"I'm going to go wait on the porch for Gramma."

"Mmm," her father mumbled, gnawing on a raw piece of pepper. "Good idea."

"Remember," Kaitlin whispered softly, leaning towards her father, "Gramma doesn't like burnt meat." She grinned as she walked around to the front of the house, kicking at each dandelion she passed.

She sank into the wooden porch swing, tucking one leg under her. She used the other foot to push herself back and forth slightly, rocking from heel to toe. Kaitlin was eagerly anticipating the arrival of her grandmother. "Gramma loves me best," she reminded herself.

Kaitlin didn't have long to wait before the huge black car streaked into view, the tires crunching the gravel of the driveway.

Kaitlin threw her arms around her grandmother and squeezed her very warmly. "Well," said Gramma, a bit winded but squeezing Kaitlin back. "I missed you too, Katie. My goodness but you're getting big." She leaned down and kissed each of Kaitlin's cheeks. Kaitlin scrunched up her face a little. Only Gramma could get away with inflicting such an indignity.

Kaitlin's dad came out from around the house, wiping his hands carefully on his barbecue apron. "Hello there, Mom Morris," he said cheerfully.

Gramma nodded at him, eyeing the streaky apron. "Hello, Daniel," she said. "I see you're barbecuing again. My luggage and presents are in the trunk. Would you be so kind as to carry them inside for me?"

He grinned ruefully and headed to the back of the car. "Of course. I was just about to ask."

"Gramma!" Anna screamed, darting across the lawn. She threw herself on the older woman, hugging her about the legs.

"Dear, dear," said Gramma. "How are you, Anna?"

"Good," said Anna, gazing up with her wide blue eyes. "I've been VERY good," she emphasized. Kaitlin snorted indelicately.

Gramma bent down to give the little girl a kiss on the forehead. As she straightened, she noticed Jane standing on the lawn.

"Hi, there," said Jane.

Gramma gave her a very slight nod and turned her attention back to Kaitlin. Jane sighed and went to help her husband with the luggage.

*   *   *

Fortunately, nothing was overcooked at dinner. Kaitlin sat on one side of Gramma, and because Anna insisted, the little girl sat on the other side of the important visitor. Both Anna and Kaitlin let the carrots pass by until Gramma spied the omission. "What do we have here?" she asked in cheerful disapproval, glancing over at Jane. "Come on, girls," said Gramma, spooning the vegetables onto their plates. "Carrots are good for your eyes. Didn't anyone ever tell you that?" Kaitlin looked over at Anna, wondering if she were going to cry.

Anna eyed the carrots doubtfully. "Why?"

Gramma shook her head. "Because they are. You ask so many questions for such a little girl."

"Everyone says that!" Anna exclaimed.

Kaitlin picked up her fork and ate a carrot deliberately under her grandmother's approving eye. Anna remained uncertain, her gaze flitting back and forth between the three carrots on her plate and Jane. But Jane stared down at her own meal.

"Good girls eat carrots," said Gramma.

Anna's eyes widened at that, looking to Jane for confirmation. Finding none, she turned back to Gramma. "Do good girls get presents?" she asked.

Laughing, Kaitlin nearly choked on her last offensive carrot. Gramma smiled benignly. "Good girls sometimes get presents," Gramma commented dryly.

Anna picked up her fork and started eating the carrots.

"You're not a bad cook, Dan," said Gramma.

Kaitlin's father looked surprised but pleased at the compliment. "Why thank you, Mom Morris. I try."

"I suppose you get a lot of practice at making the meals around here?" she inquired.

Jane's face looked a bit funny.

"We share the household duties," said Dan. Jane gave him a pointed look, and he added quickly: "Actually, Jane does more than I do, though."

"Hmm," said Gramma. "It must be difficult on the children with both parents working."

Jane's eyes flew wide open, and Kaitlin saw her Dad jump a bit. She wondered if Jane had poked him. "The children are doing just fine," he said firmly.

"Hmm," said Gramma.

After dinner, the family retired to the living room. Gramma settled in on the chesterfield with Kaitlin safely nestled under one arm. They sipped the pink lemonade Jane had made.

Anna stared with great interest at both Gramma and the box of presents. "What are those?" she asked innocently, tilting her head towards the box.

"Oh, I think you know very well what they are, Anna. They're some gifts I brought with me," Gramma answered.

"For me?"

"I'm not sure if you've been good," Gramma said sternly, softening it with a little wink. Kaitlin wondered if Gramma had noticed when Anna had dropped the last two carrots down her shirt.

The child squirmed with great impatience in her chair. "Presents, presents, presents," she chanted, kicking her legs in the air. Kaitlin willed her to be quiet. Of course, that didn't work.

Anna started an impromptu composition, a song about presents and Grammas.

Gramma squeezed Kaitlin's hand lightly. "Why don't you take our empty glasses to the kitchen to get them out of the way?"

"Sure," said Kaitlin as Gramma handed over her glass. She picked up Anna's plastic cup on the way.

"What a good girl," Kaitlin heard Gramma say behind her. "She grows more like her mother every day."

In the kitchen, Kaitlin finished the last drop of liquid in her glass and reached in to pull out a piece of ice. She sucked on it slowly, leaning against the counter. She wondered if she was the least bit like her mother. Maybe her grandmother just wanted to believe that. Shrugging, she rinsed out the glasses.

"Don't you think so?" Kaitlin could hear Gramma insisting, in the living room. "Jane?"

The response was soft and low. "I never had the chance to meet Kaitlin's mother, unfortunately. I can see a resemblance in the photos, though."

Ha, Kaitlin thought derisively.

She was surprised to hear her father speak up. "She's got her mother's eyes, there's no doubt. It's very striking."

Kaitlin peered into the chrome at the edge of the fridge to see her reflection. The image was swollen and distorted. She made a face, trying to see any resemblance to her mother's eyes.

"Did Kaitlin's mommy eat carrots?" Anna asked with great interest.

Nobody answered her.

"Carrots are good for the eyes," insisted Anna. "And brownies are good for the tummy," she added solemnly.

Kaitlin could hear Jane's warning cough.

"Katie, dear!" Gramma called. "I think it's time for the surprises."

Kaitlin spat the last bit of her ice into the sink and smoothed her shirt with her palms before going back to the living room.

Anna ran to meet her, peering at her. "Let me see your eyes!" she squealed. Kaitlin turned just slightly away from her grandmother. She scowled at the little girl, narrowing her eyes to unfriendly slits.

"Oh," said Anna, nodding. She backed over to Jane and settled in beside her mother. "I saw Kaitlin's eyes, Mommy," she whispered loudly.

Jane ruffled her curls lightly. "Yes, Anna," she said, pulling her daughter close beside her. "I noticed."

Gramma reached into the box and started handing out presents. Ever proper, she'd been certain to leave no one out. There was even a candle for Jane and a sweater for Kaitlin's father. "I imagine you usually have to buy your own clothes, Dan," Gramma mentioned casually, as she handed him the package.

There were toys and clothes for both Kaitlin and Anna, although noticeably more for Kaitlin. Anna was soon quite absorbed in trying to tug the arms and legs off her own new doll. "Gently, Anna," cautioned Gramma, with a glance at Jane.

"Yes, Gramma," said the girl, making a show of smoothing the little doll's hair. When Gramma turned her attention back to Kaitlin, Anna pulled an arm off the doll. Kaitlin watched out of the corner of her eye as Jane quickly slipped the arm and doll into a deep pocket. And before Anna's mouth was fully open in protest, Jane jumped up, pulling Anna with her. "Come on, sweetie, let's go try on your new dress."

"We'll be RIGHT BACK!" Anna shouted to Gramma.

Gramma blinked. "All right, dear. I hear you."

*   *   *

When Kaitlin got home from school the next day, Gramma was rocking on the porch swing. Cuddling up close beside her, Kaitlin smiled. "I missed you!"

"You saw me just this morning, sweetheart." But Gramma looked pleased. Kaitlin leaned back, closing her eyes, enjoying her grandmother's warmth.

"Oh, look," said Gramma. "There's that nice boy from next door." Kaitlin's eyes flew open in alarm, but Michael was just heading into his house, preoccupied with the basketball he was tossing about.

"Go get him, dear," Gramma said. "I brought him something."

"What? You brought something for Michael?"

"Yes, that dear boy. I've always liked him. Run and bring him here, will you?" Gramma said calmly, patting Kaitlin's hand.

Kaitlin could feel her heart beating faster. She bit her bottom lip nervously. "Gramma..." she began.

"Yes, Katie?" her grandmother asked curiously. "What's wrong?"

"Oh, it's just that Michael and I don't hang out these days," she stammered. "We're not exactly friends any more."

"What?" said Gramma, looking distressed. Then her expression softened. "Oh, nonsense. A nice boy like that? You're just at that age when boys and girls don't get along. It will pass. Go get him for me, please," she instructed firmly.

Kaitlin looked pleadingly at her grandmother, but saw no relenting there. Sighing, she slipped through the hole in the hedge. She straightened her shoulders, walked to the door and knocked firmly.

"Kaitlin," said Michael through the screen. He

sounded more than a little surprised to see her standing on his doorstep. He opened the door. "Did you want to come in?" he asked carefully, noting her sullen expression.

"No!" she snapped.

His eyebrows lifted slightly, but still he smiled. "Did you come to see me, or are you looking for my mother?"

"Of course!" Michael exclaimed, glancing over towards Kaitlin's house. "Is she here?"

Kaitlin nodded. "Don't ask me *why*..." she let the word drip with disdain, "but she'd like to see you. Can I tell her you're indisposed?" She smiled sweetly at him.

Michael chuckled. "Ah, Kaitlin, I could never disappoint your Gramma." He stepped out of the house, closing the door behind him.

Kaitlin turned on her heel and marched across the lawn without looking back. She could hear the hedge rustle as he followed her. "I didn't know this hole was still here!"

"It's your mom who *cuts* it," Kaitlin hissed back at him.

"Really?" He laughed. "Oh, that wacky mother."

Gramma was nowhere to be seen when they arrived back at the porch. Michael leaned against the railing, smiling cheekily at Kaitlin. "Ah, so it was all a ruse to get me over here," he murmured, his eyes twinkling.

"Don't even think it, Michael Drayson," Kaitlin said, stomping up the steps to open the door.

"Gramma!" she bellowed.

"One moment, Katie," Gramma answered from the kitchen. "I'll be right out. Why don't you entertain that nice Michael for a few minutes?"

Kaitlin blinked in genuine alarm. She called back into the house. "Hurry, Gramma!" She slouched into a deck chair and indicated another for Michael. "Sit down," she ordered.

Michael took a seat on the porch swing instead. "Yes, Katie," he mocked softly. She sunk deeper into her seat and glared at him.

"Do you remember when your Dad first made this swing, and we used to play on it?" Michael inquired, rocking back and forth a little.

Kaitlin frowned. "I remember you sat on it before the paint had even dried."

"I'll always trust you to remember the bad parts of my history, Kaitlin."

"Were there any good parts to remember?" she asked.

But just then Gramma came through the door, loaded down with a pitcher of lemonade and a tray of cookies. Michael jumped to his feet. "Let me help you with that."

"Ah, such a nice young man," Gramma smiled at him, passing him the cookies. She poured glasses of lemonade all round. Michael sat back down on the swing and Gramma seated herself beside him." You've grown so much since I was last here," she said, beaming.

"I'll have to tell my mother you said so. She's pretty obsessed with making sure I drink enough milk and eat enough vegetables."

Gramma nodded approvingly. "I've always liked your mother. It's too bad Kaitlin doesn't get similar guidance," she sighed.

"Oh, I don't know," said Michael, glancing mischievously towards Kaitlin. "I think she's growing quite nicely."

Gramma nodded. "Well, of course. She's my granddaughter." She smiled over at Kaitlin before turning back to Michael to quiz him about school and sports. He answered her questions patiently and thoroughly. He seemed genuinely fond of her.

Every now and then Michael would glance at Kaitlin's unfriendly visage, but Gramma seemed oblivious. "Here," she said eventually, handing a small package to the boy, "this is for you."

He was surprised. "You brought me a present, Gramma? That's so nice of you."

But Gramma waved her hand. "Oh, it's just a small thing. Go on, open it."

Michael unwrapped the paper to pull out a Toronto Blue Jays baseball cap. He adjusted the strap and set it on his head. "It's great! Thank you!"

"I thought of you when I saw that. I know you like to play sports."

"I do. And I'll wear this. Thank you."

Gramma nodded briskly, gathering up the dishes. "Well, thanks for coming to see this old woman. You can get back to your ball practice. I just wanted to say hello. It makes me happy to know Kaitlin has such a nice friend." She waved, then got up and carried the tray inside.

Kaitlin stood up too. "That means you can go now," she said curtly.

Michael tilted his new hat back a little, looking up at her. He got to his feet and sighed. He walked down one step, then turned back to look at her. "There's no reason why I can't actually be your friend, Kaitlin."

Disconcerted, she stared at him for a moment. "Yes, there is, Michael," she said. "I don't like you."

She stepped into her house and shut the door.

*   *   *

Kaitlin sat on the swing beside her grandmother. It was their last evening together before Gramma got back into her big long car and drove away. Crickets chirped softly. The sun had just disappeared, and a huge round moon sat just above the horizon.

"That's the biggest moon I ever saw," Kaitlin murmured, gazing at it.

Gramma nodded. "It's a big one, all right. That's what they call a harvest moon."

"Why?"

"I imagine because it's so large and bright that it's good to work under, for farmers taking in the harvest."

Kaitlin stared out at the moon. "It really does look like a face, don't you think?"

Gramma nodded. "I used to talk to the moon when I was a child and pretend it was my playmate."

Kaitlin giggled. "Your imaginary friend was the moon, Gramma?"

Gramma laughed too. "That's the truth. What strange imaginations run in this family." She shook her head, as if shaking away memories.

"You think imaginations are inherited?"

Gramma shrugged expansively. "How else can we explain it? Your mother's imaginary friend was a large purple elephant! It slept in the basement, your Mom said—because it didn't fit in her bedroom!"

"You're teasing me!"

Gramma crossed her heart.

Anna's voice called plaintively from inside the house. She was adamant about getting a tucking-in and a bedtime story from Gramma each night.

The wood creaked slightly when Gramma settled back into her seat, sighing. "What an energetic little girl that is."

"Anna thinks you're her Gramma too, you know."

Gramma leaned back with a smile. "Oh, that's okay. I'm happy to be Anna's Gramma as well." She paused. "After all, she's my granddaughter's sister."

"Half-sister," Kaitlin corrected automatically.

"You should consider yourself lucky to have any sort of sister at all, dear."

Kaitlin scrunched up her face doubtfully. "Lucky?" She glanced at her grandmother. "She's very loud and destructive and...annoying," Kaitlin ended a bit lamely.

Gramma chuckled. "That's the role of little sisters, dear. But a sister is something to treasure throughout life."

Kaitlin hesitated for a moment, then ventured: "But you don't like Jane, do you, Gramma?"

Gramma was quiet for a moment. Kaitlin could tell her grandmother wasn't sure how to answer the question. "Oh, Kaitlin. I guess I just still wish sometimes that it was my daughter here with her child and her husband. I know it's selfish of me."

"But I wish that too," Kaitlin interjected softly.

Gramma nodded, staring downward at the floor of

the porch. The swing rocked very gently, back and forth. "I know you do, sweetie." Gramma paused, as if she were still searching for words. "But things aren't always the way we would want them, and we need to accept that, I guess."

Kaitlin pushed at the floor with her heel, rocking the swing with a bit more energy.

Gramma lightly stroked Kaitlin's hair. "Speaking of sisters, Katie, when your mom was small, you know, she used to want a sister desperately. I'm sure she's happy to know that you have one."

Kaitlin snuggled into Gramma's warmth. "Do you think she knows about the stuff going on with us now?" she asked.

Gramma paused, contemplating. "Well, dear, I don't know whether your mom can watch us minute-by-minute in heaven or not."

"Like on TV screens?"

"I just don't know if it's like that. Television screens, my goodness. You amuse me no end, Katie. But you know what...if your mom couldn't watch what was going on down here with her family, I know she'd at least be asking for very regular updates!"

Kaitlin smiled, trying to imagine that. Gramma continued: "So, yes, I'm sure she does know what a bright and lovely girl you're becoming, dear. I'm sure she's aware of that."

Kaitlin blushed. "Aw, Gramma. You're pretty biased about that, I think." She was flattered nonetheless.

Gramma shook her head. "I'm being absolutely objective here. If anyone ever says differently, you send them to me, and I'll set them straight."

Kaitlin leaned up and kissed her grandmother's soft wrinkled cheek. "Okay, I will."

Gramma slipped her hand into a pocket of her apron and brought out a small blue box. "I have one more thing for you, sweetie."

"Oh, Gramma," Kaitlin protested. "You've given me enough already!"

"Well, this is a little different. Open it."

Obediently, Kaitlin pried open the box. Nestled on the velvet was a silver bracelet. It was decorated with tiny charms in the shapes of dogs of various breeds.

"Ooh," she breathed, stroking the cool silver coat of a miniature poodle.

"Katie," said Gramma with a smile, watching her closely, "this was your mother's when she was a girl, and before that, it was mine."

Kaitlin felt a warmth spreading in her chest and a pricking sensation behind her eyes. She blinked the feeling back. "Thank you," she said. She held the bracelet very tightly in her hand.

"There, there," Gramma said. "Let me help you put it on."

"I'll miss you when you leave," Kaitlin said as her grandmother fastened the bracelet.

"Shush," said Gramma, trying for her no-nonsense voice. "I'll miss you too, but I'll be back before you know it. And in the meantime, young lady, I'll be expecting some letters from you."

"Yes, Gramma."

Kaitlin hugged her tightly.

Eight

Click, click, click... Glenn tapped his pencil lightly against the side of his desk, letting the metallic band hit against the wooden desk edge. His body swayed slightly, as if he was keeping time to the beat of some invisible band. He turned slightly in his seat, meeting Kaitlin's gaze. He suddenly gave her a bold wink.

Warmth flooded her face, and she abruptly switched her attention to a nondescript scratch on the surface of her own desk. She glanced discreetly over at Tracy to see if her friend had noticed, but Tracy's head was down as she doodled on the back of a notebook. Tap, tap, tap...went Glenn's pencil.

"All right, class." Ms. Manon got up from her desk and pulled a bulky yellow envelope out of a drawer. "I've got your science tests marked," she said briskly, walking towards the students. There were quiet groans from all over the class, and Ms. Manon smiled. "Come now, they weren't so bad." Moving swiftly about the class, she handed out the papers, her short heels clacking as they made contact with the hard linoleum. The efficiently rustled papers partially hid Ms. Manon's murmured comments to each student. "Better, Glenn," said the teacher, laying his paper down in front of him.

Chuck peered over Glenn's shoulder. "68 per cent," he mumbled. "I just got 60."

Tracy made a face at her own paper. "Well, 72," she said, waving the test at Kaitlin before turning it over and starting with fresh doodles on the back, mainly her own name alongside the names of movie stars. Then she'd enclose them in large wildly coloured hearts.

"Well done, Kaitlin," said Ms. Manon. A big 90 per cent was written across the top of the first sheet of the test. Kaitlin flipped the pages, looking for her error. "Cytoplasm!" she muttered. "How could I forget that was part of a cell?" She tapped herself on the forehead, sighing.

"Excellent work, Winter," said Ms. Manon, smiling with approval at the tall girl sitting up so straight in her seat.

"Thank you, Ms. Manon." Winter inclined her head at the compliment. Kaitlin stared at the back of her head, waiting for her to turn around. Growing impatient, she coughed softly. Winter rotated in her chair, raising an eyebrow. Kaitlin nodded her head in the direction of Winter's test. Winter gestured similarly back at Kaitlin's paper. Then they both held their pages up with the written sides hidden from view. "One, two, three," they mouthed at each other and flipped them over at exactly the same moment in a well-rehearsed move. The mark on Winter's paper read 96 per cent. Kaitlin stuck out her tongue, and Winter stifled a laugh.

While Ms. Manon was speaking with another student, Winter turned around and whispered an explanation: "I studied for two hours the night before."

Kaitlin blinked. "Why? The test wasn't that hard. I didn't study at all, and I got 90 per cent."

Winter nodded. "Yes, but I did study," she said, emphasizing each word, "and I got 96 per cent!" She flashed a wide grin at Kaitlin before turning again towards the front of the class.

"Man," joked Glenn, "I'm going to have to start cheating off of Winter." Then he looked over at Kaitlin and drawled: "'Course, I'd be willing to cheat off of you too, Kaitlin, so don't get jealous."

Winter half-snorted a laugh but kept working on the math assignment.

"That's *highly unlikely*," Kaitlin stressed for Winter's benefit.

"*Improbable*, even," returned Winter without looking back.

"Do you want to come with me next time I visit my Mom at her new house?" Tracy whispered.

"Sure, okay," Kaitlin nodded, curious. Her friend's face was downcast. Sighing to herself, Kaitlin wished she could tell Tracy it was all going to be okay. She leaned over impulsively to pet Fred, who was perched on the corner of Tracy's desk.

Giggling, Tracy started another doodle. First, she drew a big pink heart. Then she picked up a green marker and wrote in neat letters "Best Friends Always." She tilted the paper proudly towards Kaitlin.

"Right," Kaitlin whispered.

"Girls are so lame," complained Chuck. "Will you be my best friend?" he mocked. "Hey, Glenn," he continued, in a high falsetto, "will you be my best friend?"

Glenn laughed, his voice deep and full. "Who are my other choices?"

Winter turned slowly and deliberately in her chair. She leaned her elbow over the back of her seat, then crossed one long leg over the other. "Chuckie boy," she said, lowering her voice so it sounded particularly dangerous, "watch your step, hmm?" She fixed her gaze on him and whispered in a voice that carried well across the room. "We both know I can still beat you up."

Flushing, Chuck sank down in his seat while the other boys laughed loudly. Glenn applauded while Kaitlin and Tracy giggled. Winter swung back around and diligently picked up her pencil.

When Ms. Manon raised her head, her eyes widened in surprise at the uproar in her classroom. "Is anyone besides Winter actually doing their math assignment?" she asked.

Chuck sat up straight in his desk and waved his hand. "I'm doing my assignment, Ms. Manon!" he announced, straight-faced.

"Uh-huh," said the unimpressed teacher. "Should I come check on your progress then?" she asked, taking a step in Chuck's direction.

"Oh! I need a few more minutes, I think, Ms. Manon."

"I see," she said dryly. "I'm sure you do. Everybody get to work, please." She sat down at her desk and started writing in her lesson planner.

Kaitlin reluctantly turned her attention to the math problem in front of her.

Click, click, click, went Glenn's pencil, on the side of his desk.

*   *   *

Running her fingertips along the hard cool rock, Kaitlin could feel the delicate edge of the tombstone's engraving. *Andrew Johnson, beloved son, 1899-1912*, said the carefully styled writing.

She tried to imagine the unknown young boy and the short life he had lived. "I wonder what he died of," she mused, caressing the stone. "Maybe tuberculosis," she added.

"Why tuberculosis?" Winter inquired, with a lift of her eyebrows.

"He had to die of something, didn't he?"

"I doubt it was old age."

"That would be *dubious*," Kaitlin responded with an arch look.

Winter had a wicked gleam in her eyes. "Perhaps he was murdered," she whispered dramatically. "Because he knew too much," she added, emphasizing each word. "And then, the murderers slipped the evidence of the secrets into his coffin, to be buried forever with this poor unfortunate boy." Her eyes were wide with assumed horror as her gaze travelled slowly between Kaitlin and Tracy.

"What secrets?" gasped Tracy, staring uncertainly at Winter.

"I do not know," Winter replied slowly, as if considering the matter. She pressed her toe slightly into the earth, eyeing the ground in deep contemplation. Her head flew up suddenly and she leaned very close to Tracy. "That is why we have to dig Andrew up," she hissed, her voice deep and sinister.

Tracy took a quick step back. "You're so sick!" she exclaimed in disgust.

Kaitlin giggled, which rather spoiled the moment.

Tracy shook her head ruefully. "You're so awful, Winter."

The sound of Winter's full laugh carried robustly over the small century-old graveyard.

After laying some freshly picked wildflowers on Andrew's grave, the girls sat down on the grass beside the stone. Kaitlin cleared her throat importantly. "I've gathered you together today, because the time has come for revenge."

"Oh my," Winter blinked, her tone wry. "Yet another murder? That would be *excessive*."

Kaitlin frowned. "As I was saying, the time has come for revenge on our arch-enemy Michael Drayson for all the evils he has done us."

"Excuse me, Kaitlin. Since when is he my arch-enemy? I barely know the fellow, and he seems rather decent, really."

"That, my dear, is a clever front to mask his truly *horrific* nature."

Tracy nodded vigorously in support. But she whispered as an aside to Winter, "Don't you think he's kind of cute?"

"Oh, I'd say," Winter said. She gave a whistle of appreciation.

"Blech," said Kaitlin, scowling at them both before starting again. "You two are my best friends in the whole world," she explained carefully. "Michael is my *avowed*…" Kaitlin glanced at Winter, stressing the word, "enemy, and I need to know if I can count on you in my time of need."

"I'm here for you," Tracy said fervently. "I will do whatever you want to see that your enemy is punished for his wrongs." She crossed her heart, then double-crossed it for emphasis. Kaitlin nodded approvingly at the enthusiastic effort.

Winter rolled her eyes and sighed. "You know, I prefer to use my considerable powers for good. Can you promise it will at least be *notably* amusing?"

"*Decidedly* so," nodded Kaitlin. "It will be *vastly* amusing."

"Oh, all right," Winter agreed. "What's the plan?"

"Well…" said Kaitlin, her voice slow and measured. "I've found over the years, in my combat with Michael, that it's very difficult to upset him."

"I just hate those stable, even-tempered boys!" Winter mocked, throwing her hands into the air.

Tracy poked her, giggling. Kaitlin growled.

"Oh, do go on," chuckled Winter. "Your enemy is the *unflappable* Michael Drayson. But now you want to flap him, so to speak."

In spite of herself, Kaitlin grinned. "Yes, that's the goal. To seriously flap Michael."

Tracy screwed up her face, not getting it. "What?" she asked plaintively.

"We need to do something to get at Michael," Kaitlin explained. "Something he'll take seriously."

"Like what?"

"Indeed," agreed Winter. "Do tell us your incredible

plan, Kaitlin."

"Well..." Kaitlin continued, "it occurs to me that to hurt Michael, we need to take something of value away from him."

"Ah. We're going to pick the lock on his school locker and steal his basketball." Winter grinned.

"Hardly." Kaitlin paused. "I want to take away his girlfriend."

Winter let out a hoot of laughter. "Shelley? Oh, Kaitlin." She poked her friend lightly. "You're jealous."

"Don't be insulting. This is a very good plan."

"Oh, of course it is."

"How?" asked Tracy, with a furrowed brow as she pondered the matter. "How will we take her away from him?" She didn't seem opposed to the idea.

"Well," Kaitlin said generously, "what would you suggest?"

Scrunching up her face, Tracy absently picked grass as she tried to come up with a solution. "We could tell her bad things about him so she wouldn't like him."

"Bah," said Winter. "I'm sure she's aware of the *animosity* Kaitlin has for Michael. She probably wouldn't believe us. Besides, Grade Eight girls wouldn't listen to anything we have to say. It's a matter of principle. Class segregation."

"My thoughts exactly," Kaitlin agreed. "Winter, how do you think we should go about this?"

But Winter just waved her hand airily in Kaitlin's direction. "You go, girl."

Kaitlin smiled and reached over to pat the gravestone. "Andrew," she said simply.

"What?" exclaimed Tracy, with a look of horror in her eyes.

Kaitlin grinned in barely suppressed triumph. "We are going to make Shelley fall for our dear friend Andrew."

"Heaven help us," groaned Winter. With her knees drawn up, she lay very still in the grass. Her quizzical gaze slid between the old gravestone and Kaitlin's calm face. She glanced over at Tracy, who was dissecting a dandelion. Sighing, she watched some big fluffy clouds float by. "I know I'll be sorry for asking, but why do we want to set up our favourite dead boy with Ms. Grade Eight Popularity?"

Kaitlin blinked, as if the answer was self-evident. "Well, for starters, Andrew's apt to go along with whatever we suggest. Personally, I find live boys at best very uncooperative."

Winter eyed Kaitlin. "I'm already regretting any *peripheral* involvement on my part in this effort, incidentally."

Kaitlin waited calmly.

Sighing just once, for effect, Winter shrugged. "Oh, fine. So how will our dear friend Andrew lure his victim, then? I doubt it will be his youthful good looks?"

"On the contrary," Kaitlin protested, fondly patting the headstone, "I've always imagined Andrew to be a rather charming young man."

"With curly black hair and gorgeous green eyes," Tracy murmured dreamily, her fingers lightly caressing a ragged dandelion. "That's what I picture."

"I'm more of a sucker for big brown eyes, myself," Winter murmured. "Not that there's anything wrong with green eyes."

"Hey, I have green eyes," protested Kaitlin.

"And fine eyes they are." Winter grinned widely. Still laughing, she pursued the discussion of Andrew's virtues. "I suppose he's tall and athletic?" she asked skeptically.

Kaitlin nodded with a serene smile. "But not too athletic, and he never watches hockey on television." Sounding very sincere, she specified the details while Tracy murmured in agreement. Warming up, Kaitlin continued: "Plus, he's very intelligent and likes to paint and draw. He also composes songs on his guitar."

"He's very sensitive," whispered Tracy, eyeing the tombstone with appreciation.

Winter shook her head. "I realize, of course, that I'm surrounded by insanity." She squinted off into the distance over Kaitlin's shoulder. "Am I seeing things, or are a couple of those so-called uncooperative boys of our acquaintance heading this way?"

Kaitlin's eyes narrowed. "Boys," she muttered scornfully, as Glenn and Chuck came into view. "What are they doing here?"

Winter lifted her palms skywards. "Beats me. We're rather out of the way here. Either they're stalking us, or..." her eyebrows raised once, expressively, in Tracy's direction.

Sure enough, Tracy blushed deeply in an admission of guilt. Kaitlin poked her friend with considerable force.

"I saw them when I was walking over here," Tracy stammered. "They asked me where I was going." Her eyes darted in nervous appeal between Winter and Kaitlin.

Chuck waved. Glenn surveyed the scene in the old

graveyard with appreciation. "A bit morbid, are we girls?" He tapped lightly at the edge of Kaitlin's hat as he took a place on the grass beside her.

Chuck walked about, looking for a clear spot of grass.

"Don't step on the grave," Kaitlin hissed in fierce rebuke.

Startled, Chuck glanced in surprise down at his feet. He quickly stepped off, then sprawled a safe distance away. "Why?" he asked defensively.

Kaitlin pulled herself up, gazing down at him. "It's disrespectful."

"Really?" asked Chuck, eyeing Kaitlin uncertainly. He threw a glance in Glenn's direction.

Glenn shrugged nonchalantly. "Don't ask me. I'm not a graveyard regular myself."

"I think there's an element of danger, as well," Winter mused. "That's part of the reason."

Suddenly, Tracy squeaked softly. "Ghosts?" Her eyes were very wide.

The boys laughed, but Winter just smiled and shook her head slightly. "Nothing so *intriguing*," she returned. "However, I've heard it's conceivable that the old coffins can collapse, and the earth could give way above, if you're so unlucky as to be standing there."

"Wow," said Chuck, impressed. "That is so cool."

"It is also highly *improbable*," Kaitlin said dryly, watching Winter from half-closed eyelids.

Winter was unperturbed. "No doubt. But doesn't it make you think twice?" She leaned over and tapped Chuck on the knee. He blushed profusely.

"I'd love to see that," Glenn said. He turned towards Chuck. "Why don't you keep walking on those graves, eh, Chuck? I need more amusement in my life."

He sat down beside Tracy. "So what were you all whispering about, when we arrived, hmm?" Glenn asked Tracy.

Kaitlin's eyes flashed in sudden alarm, but under the influence of Glenn's dark green gaze, Tracy nearly gushed, "We're trying to set Shelley up with Andrew." Then catching the full force of Kaitlin's glare, she mouthed a silent "Ooh," and shrank down apologetically.

Glenn's eyebrows came together. "Andrew?" he asked, perplexed, visibly turning the name over in his head. His eyes were drawn suddenly to the words on the headstone. He glanced at the girls, then back to the name. Leaning back on his elbows, he raised a brow in Kaitlin's direction. His voice was warm with laughter. "Oh, Kaitlin, Kaitlin, Kaitlin."

The air seemed oddly heavy as it hung over the graveyard. Kaitlin shifted uncomfortably, feeling the sharp edge of the gravestone press into her side. She moved just slightly away from the stone.

Tracy looked subdued and chagrined, although Chuck seemed merely confused. "Uh," he said. "You lost me."

Tracy suddenly clasped her hands in front of her and adopted her most cajoling expression as she tried to redeem herself. "Of course, it's an absolute secret. We'll only tell you the details if you cross your heart and hope to die, stick a needle in your eye."

"Good thing *you* didn't make such a promise, hmm?"

Winter murmured in a soft aside to Tracy.

Kaitlin concentrated on Tracy's unwelcome offer. "What! Of course, they can't know the secret!"

Chuck flushed in indignation at the exclusion. "Hey, tell me the secret."

Glenn leaned closer. "Come now, Kaitlin. Tell us your secrets. Maybe we can help you."

"I highly doubt that you could help us."

Winter reached over and tapped Kaitlin's running shoe. "These fellows could be useful as we *orchestrate* this unusual romance." Winter turned towards Glenn and continued blithely: "We are planning to make Shelley fall for our dead friend Andrew, thereby breaking up her association with Michael Drayson."

Kaitlin narrowed her eyes to dark slits and glared at Winter.

"Hmm," said Glenn, contemplating the information. "It's an interesting, although unusual plan. Myself, I'm partial to dating live people."

Kaitlin rolled her eyes.

"Oh no, we're just going to pretend Andrew's a live boy and try to use him to lure away Shelley," Tracy explained earnestly.

"Why not use a live guy?" Chuck asked.

Winter grinned slowly. "Well, we'd need a volunteer. Moreover, we'd need someone who's up to umm...luring Shelley." Her eyes twinkled mischievously. "Chuck, were you volunteering?"

His face instantly turned bright red. "No!" he exclaimed loudly.

Glenn eyed the girls. "And why are we doing this?

Which one of you is after Michael?"

"Idiot!" Kaitlin almost shouted. "We don't like Michael, we hate him."

"I see," said Glenn, watching her closely for a moment. He leaned over and plucked the dandelion that Tracy had been molesting and threw it on the grave along with the other assorted wildflowers.

"Why?" interjected Chuck blankly. "Michael's okay." He glanced quickly towards Glenn, as if for confirmation.

"I never minded him myself." Glenn turned to Winter. "You hate Michael?" he asked mildly.

She shrugged noncommittally. "It's one of those group-dislike things."

But Glenn only chuckled. "So," he said, in a surprisingly helpful tone. He rubbed his palms together. "How do we get Shelley interested in old Andrew, hmm?" Kaitlin frowned warningly, but Glenn seemed genuinely interested in the plot.

"We can write her notes, from him," suggested Tracy eagerly.

Kaitlin tried to ignore the boys. "To *pique* her interest," she said pointedly to Winter.

"It's going to be a bit tricky leaving notes without being spotted, I think," Winter mused.

Chuck coughed. Everyone turned to look at him. "Email," he blurted out.

"Hmm?" asked Kaitlin, squinting at him. Chuck blushed again.

Winter nodded. "That's better than messing about with actual notes. We'll create an account for the boy of our dreams, and he can start emailing Shelley."

Kaitlin thought about that for a moment, before giving her a nod of approval. "Then all we have to do is get Shelley's email address."

"Look at that," Glenn murmured smoothly. "We're helping already."

*   *   *

The next day at school, Chuck bent his red-haired head over the computer keyboard. He sighed in frustration. "I know how to do this," he muttered irritably.

Tracy hovered closely behind him, leaning over his shoulder. She seemed to be watching Chuck, rather than the computer monitor. Kaitlin paced restlessly behind them.

"Bah," said Winter with good-natured impatience. "You may know how to do this, but I know how to do it quickly. Move over." She poked Chuck in the arm, not lightly.

Grumbling, he relinquished the seat to Winter. "Here you go then, Ms. Brains."

Kaitlin heard a low whistle and spun around to see Glenn sauntering into the computer lab. "Hey, Chuck," he said. "Don't you know you're in way over your head with these girls?" He folded his arms and leaned casually against a filing cabinet. He cocked an eyebrow in Kaitlin's direction. "Working on your sweet revenge plan, I assume?"

Kaitlin eyed him carefully. "You don't need to stick around, you know. We've got it under control."

"No doubt. But there's nothing I'd rather do then

watch you girls stir up trouble. Besides," he said, tapping his fingers on the top of the cabinet, "I'll be your lookout. You never know, a bunch of other kids might want to geek out on the computer over lunch hour."

"There," said Winter briskly, flashing a triumphant look first towards Chuck, then over to Kaitlin. "Andrew Johnson has an email address that doesn't trace back to any of us." She stood up and wiped her hands on her shiny purple pants. "There's my contribution to the revenge," she said wryly.

Kaitlin brought her palms together in pantomimed applause. Then a silence descended upon the group. Glenn tapped lightly on the file cabinet.

"Well?" demanded Winter with a slight frown at Kaitlin. "Don't you want to send an email?" She gestured towards the computer.

"Oh," said Kaitlin, feeling a bit uncertain. She swallowed hard. "Of course," she said, trying to make her voice sound firm. She slipped into the proffered chair and pulled the keyboard closer to her.

Dear Shelley, she typed slowly.

"Dear Shelley, I love you so much," Chuck suggested mockingly in a high falsetto.

Glenn laughed.

Kaitlin's fingers slipped from the keyboard. She turned around in her seat. "Okay, let's make it clear. Boys aren't allowed to help write the letters. Keep quiet."

Tracy giggled and patted Chuck's arm consolingly. "There, there," she said to him soothingly.

Kaitlin turned her attention back to the computer then began to type.

I hope you don't mind, but I wanted to write and say hello to you. I've noticed you around town, but we've never got a chance to actually talk.

Sliding behind Kaitlin, Glenn read the screen. "That's really lame," he whispered.

Kaitlin ignored him. "Winter," she said, "did you want to type something?"

"I never meant to get this involved as it is. Go ahead."

Tracy leaned across Chuck to suggest brightly, "Why don't you write about how pretty Shelley is?"

Kaitlin frowned. "She's not pretty."

"She certainly is," Glenn countered.

Tossing her ponytail, Tracy sighed impatiently. "It doesn't matter what we think. Andrew likes her, so he needs to explain why."

Kaitlin nodded at the reasoning and resumed typing.

Maybe you didn't notice me, because you seem to have piles of friends about all the time, but I think you're really pretty. I hope you're not mad at me for saying that.

I'm in Grade 10 at Sir John A. Macdonald High School across town. I know what school you go to, but I don't know what grade you're in.

I like sports and drawing, and I play guitar. What do you like to do?"

"This guy's really prissy," Glenn complained.

Kaitlin turned and kicked him in the shin.

"Ow!" Glenn exclaimed, more in surprise than pain, as he rubbed his leg with a rueful grin.

"Andrew isn't prissy," Kaitlin muttered. "Besides, you guys are supposed to keep quiet."

Winter whispered to Glenn, "Yes, can't you behave decently like Andrew?"

"We love Andrew," Tracy said fervently.

Shaking his head in disbelief, Glenn walked back to slouch against the filing cabinet.

Kaitlin sighed, rereading the letter. "Is that enough?"

"You've got to ask her to write back," Winter pointed out logically.

"Right," said Kaitlin, tapping at the keys.

Well, Shelley, I don't want to bother you too much today. If you want to, I'd really like it if you email me back.
Your admirer,
Andrew

Kaitlin moved the computer cursor to Send on the screen. She looked into Tracy's bright eyes, and her friend nodded eagerly.

Kaitlin turned to look at Winter questioningly.

"It's your call, baby," her friend said softly, with a half-shrug.

Kaitlin squirmed a bit. She willed herself to think of her campaign against the detestable Michael Drayson. She paused, took a very deep breath and hit Send.

Tracy clasped her hands to her heart melodramatically. "This is so exciting," she breathed. "I wish Andrew would email me."

Nine

Walking home from school, Kaitlin swung her arms with extra vigour. The air felt crisp and cool against her face.

Kaitlin resumed her normal sullen expression as she passed by the Draysons' house. She glanced over the hedge and saw Mrs. Drayson in the backyard. The woman looked up at that very moment and waved energetically in Kaitlin's direction. Kaitlin returned the wave.

Luckily, Michael wasn't around. Of course, there was no way he could already know about Andrew's email, yet the whole plot had given her an unpleasant nervous feeling in her stomach. She wasn't going to back out now though. Michael would be very sorry indeed, she told herself.

She slipped her key from about her neck and unlocked the front door. After dumping her backpack on the kitchen table, she pulled out her heavy science textbook, then poured herself a glass of milk. She sat sipping the milk as she tried to memorize the defining characteristics of arachnids.

A few moments later, another key rattled in the lock. Her father, Jane and Anna poured into the house. Anna was dancing around, pretending to be a ballerina, or more specifically, a loud, unsteady, clumsy ballerina.

Anna peered at the open pages, then immediately let out a full-volume scream. Jane dashed into the kitchen.

"Spiders!" the little girl screeched. "Spiders in the book!"

Jane pressed a hand against her heart. "Goodness, Anna. Don't screech like that." She glanced at the textbook. "They're just pictures of spiders, Anna," she pointed out mildly.

"Pictures of spiders!" Anna yelled loudly. "Pictures of spiders in the book!"

Kaitlin rolled her eyes and took another drink of milk.

Her dad ruffled her hair. "Hi, Katie. Whatcha doing?"

She smoothed her palms against her hair, trying to reflatten it. "Studying. I don't read up on arachnids for fun, you know."

He laughed at that but still looked a bit mystified. "It's just that I seldom see you studying. Do you have a test?"

"Unfortunately."

"Oh," he said, pulling up a chair across from her. "Are you worried about it, then?"

"About the test? I just want to beat Winter, is all," she explained bluntly.

Her dad smacked his palm against the tabletop while he laughed. "I like that Winter," he said simply.

"She's my second-best friend," Kaitlin said. She wondered why that made him laugh harder. Just then the doorbell rang, one loud peal.

"I'll get it! I'll get it! I'll get it!" yelled Anna, running towards the front door.

"Anna's going to get the door," Kaitlin's dad remarked dryly.

"So it seems," said Jane, smiling at him.

Kaitlin frowned. She could hear Anna struggling with the doorknob. The little girl shrieked.

Jane and Kaitlin's father exchanged glances. "Who is it, Anna?" Jane called out.

"Brownies!" Anna screamed back.

Shocked, they erupted from their chairs to dash into the living room.

Anna was outside the door, lifting a plate of brownies covered in plastic wrap off the front porch. Running past her, Kaitlin looked out into the yard, but she couldn't see anyone. "Brownies, brownies!" Anna shrieked in delight, hugging the plate close to her chest.

"Can I read that card?" Kaitlin asked, astonished.

Anna danced around for a few minutes. But finally she handed the small white envelope over to Kaitlin, although she kept a firm hold on the brownies.

The name "Anna" was written in careful block letters on the front of the envelope. Kaitlin unfolded a small note written in the same nondescript printing. She read it aloud.

Dear Anna:
Here are those brownies I told you I'd make you.
Sorry I left for heaven so quickly. Remember to be a
good girl.
Mrs. Telgord

"I knew it!" exclaimed Anna in glee. "She promised!"

Kaitlin felt a little shiver go through her. She stared at her dad, who shook his head in confusion. Jane looked similarly perplexed. "Who...?"

"I have no idea!" gasped Kaitlin, running down the steps and out into the street. She looked both ways but couldn't see anything out of the ordinary. Shrugging, she walked back up the stairs to the porch.

Anna was already munching on a brownie. "You won't find her."

"What?" said Kaitlin, blinking at her sister. "Who won't I find?" She waited, hoping against hope that the girl would actually shed some light on the mystery.

Anna stomped her small foot impatiently. "Mrs. Telgord," she said, with a note of exasperation in her voice.

"Why not?"

Anna handed her a brownie. She patted Kaitlin's hand lightly. "Mrs. Telgord's in heaven."

*   *   *

On Saturday, the autumn air felt extra-crisp. Kaitlin shivered slightly and pulled her jean jacket over her purple T-shirt. Keeping one toe on the porch, she pushed the porch swing slightly back and forth, lingering over a persistent creak. She glanced at her watch. Tracy and her mother were late, as usual.

"Kaitlin!" boomed a deep voice from the next yard. She dashed over to Mr. Drayson. She peered at the big man over the hedge. "Hi, Mr. Drayson!"

"Hey, Katie," he said as he tossed a chocolate bar in her direction over the hedge.

Kaitlin quickly dropped the strap of her backpack and caught the candy. "That was too heavy in my pocket," he said. "Will you do me a favour and take it off my hands?"

Kaitlin cocked her head at him, grinning. "Anything to help you out. I know how heavy chocolate can get."

He laughed. "That's what my wife says, anyhow." Kaitlin liked the big deep sound of this good-natured man. Mr. and Mrs. Drayson are such nice people, Kaitlin thought suddenly to herself. It was unfortunate that her arch-enemy happened to be their son.

Reaching over the hedge, Mr. Drayson plucked a quarter out of the air, just above Kaitlin's ear. She shook her head at him, laughing. "Silly."

Mr. Drayson pretended to look offended. "Silly!" he exclaimed gruffly. "That's what you think. You'll change your tune when I pull a rabbit out of your ear!"

Kaitlin considered that. She peered over the hedge, but no furry animals were in sight. "Do it!" she challenged.

He cleared his throat importantly and reached out his arm, poised to demonstrate this superior magic trick. But then he paused, and his look turned sheepish. He dropped his arm and pursed his lips ruefully. "Can I get back to you on that?"

Kaitlin giggled.

Laughing, he slipped the quarter back into his shirt pocket. He eyed her backpack curiously. "So what are you up to this fine day, hmm? It's not a school day, you know."

She made a face. "I wouldn't get confused about something like that! I'm going to visit my friend Tracy at her mom's new house." She slipped her newly acquired chocolate bar into a pocket of her backpack.

Mr. Drayson nodded solemnly. "It's good to have friends," he said, simply.

"Like my dad?" asked Kaitlin.

He smiled at her. "Sure. Your dad is a great guy."

"I'm sure he likes you too," she assured him seriously.

"I'm glad to hear that, Katie. I'd be most disturbed if it were otherwise." He gestured with a wave of his hand towards her driveway. "I think your friend is here," he said. "Have fun, eh, kiddo?"

"Thanks for the chocolate bar! Bye!" Kaitlin called out to Mr. Drayson as she dashed back to her porch. She pulled opened the door and yelled, "They're here, bye!"

There was some sort of muffled response, so she pulled the door shut and ran to jump in the back seat of the car. Jane drew back a curtain and waved as the car pulled out of the driveway. Kaitlin pretended not to see, but Tracy responded with enthusiastic waving. "Bye, bye!" she yelled loudly at Kaitlin's house before rolling up the window.

Kaitlin turned her eyes to Tracy's mother. "Hi, Mrs. Leeland."

The woman glanced at Kaitlin in the mirror. "Hello, Kaitlin," she said quietly. Mrs. Leeland's face seemed thinner, but she was wearing more make-up, and her hair was blonder and curlier than it used to be.

Tracy lapsed into silence.

The atmosphere was heavy, too quiet. The air

seemed extra-thick, and Kaitlin wondered if she should open a window. She pushed a button on the door, but nothing happened. She sighed and squirmed in the silence. "I like your hair, Mrs. Leeland," she blurted out finally.

Mrs. Leeland looked in the mirror again and touched her well-manicured fingers to her hair. "Why, thank you. I think it suits me too." She paused for a moment then glanced at Kaitlin again. "You might have to stop calling me Mrs. Leeland soon, though."

Kaitlin blinked. She didn't know Tracy's mom's first name and wondered if she should ask. But the woman continued: "I might go back to my birth name. Lumb."

"Lumb," Kaitlin repeated uncertainly.

"Oh, I know, it's awful. I never liked that name. That's why I can't decide which name I want to use, Leeland or Lumb." She smiled wryly, glancing into the side mirror as she changed lanes. "At least I can keep the same initials. Small mercies."

Kaitlin heard a small sniffing sound and realized that Tracy must be crying in the front seat.

"Sheesh," said Tracy's mother irritably. "I don't need any more of that."

Tracy cried louder. Kaitlin shrank down uncomfortably. She stared at a bit of torn vinyl trim hanging from the back of the front seat.

No one spoke.

Tracy's mother lived in one part of an old house that had been converted into apartments. The place seemed a bit run down and was sparsely furnished. But fresh pink carnations decorated a small round kitchen table, almost matching the frilly lace curtains hanging over the small windows.

Tracy's mother retreated further into the apartment, and Kaitlin and Tracy sat glumly at either end of an ivory-coloured leather sofa. "Where do you sleep when you stay here?" Kaitlin whispered to Tracy.

Tracy gestured to their current seat. "She makes me hide all my stuff in the daytime. She hates clutter," Tracy added tonelessly.

Kaitlin sighed and rummaged in her backpack for the chocolate bar. "Do you want half? It's from Mr. Drayson."

Tracy eyed it for a moment. "Okay," she agreed finally. "Why did he give it to you?"

"Just 'cause he's nice, I guess. He always has candy in his pockets. Anna calls him The Candy Man."

"Don't you feel weird taking candy from Michael's family?"

"No!" Kaitlin denied, almost too quickly. "Let's think of it as one less chocolate bar for Michael." She laughed to herself. "Think about it. Our enemy could have been enjoying this candy treat at this very moment if I hadn't intervened!"

"Mmm," agreed Tracy, popping a square into her mouth. Her smile didn't quite reach her eyes.

Kaitlin didn't pay much attention to the sound of a vehicle outside, but when the noise got so loud that the windows in the apartment started to vibrate, she sat up in real alarm. "What's that?" she demanded, wide-eyed.

Tracy sighed and slumped down further. "Probably Terence," she said in a low voice. "My mom's friend.

I'm afraid he's going to be her boyfriend."

Kaitlin darted over to the window. A man dressed entirely in dark-coloured clothing, from jeans to helmet to leather jacket to sunglasses, was revving the engine of his bike in the driveway. "He's all in black. He looks like a bad guy."

Suddenly, the man looked up at the house. Kaitlin jumped back in alarm. A moment later, there was a knock at the door, then he walked in, dumping his helmet and saddlebag on the kitchen counter. He peeled off his jacket, and Kaitlin stared at him in surprise. He had bright blue eyes and rather long, blonde, curly hair. And he looked like he was about seventeen years old. Kaitlin blinked hard.

"Hi, Tracy," the guy said with a ready smile.

Kaitlin stood awkwardly beside the window. The guy looked curiously at Kaitlin. She realized she was staring and glanced appealingly at Tracy. Tracy didn't look up.

"Hello!" he finally exclaimed, extending his hand to Kaitlin. "I'm Terry."

Kaitlin looked helplessly at Tracy again, to no avail. The guy still had his hand out. "Um, Kaitlin," she said. She reluctantly put her hand in his, and he shook it vigorously. "Nice to meet you! Do you like root beer?"

"Um," said Kaitlin, "I guess so."

"Perfect. I just never know what to think of people who don't like root beer. I mean, it's a great drink. So don't you think there has to be something suspicious about people who say they don't like it?"

Kaitlin smiled a little. "I guess so." She cleared her throat and resumed her more hostile expression. "You were making a lot of noise with your motorcycle."

"Oh, I know," he said. "I was trying to listen to it."

Kaitlin squinted at him. "I'm sure the rest of the block was trying *not* to listen to it."

He laughed, shaking his head. "You're cute," he said, grinning. "I love witty females who drink root beer. Really, I think I might have a rattle in there somewhere. I heard some kind of noise on the bike." He whistled under his breath as he dug in his saddlebag. He plopped a bag of cheezies and a couple of cans of pop on the coffee table.

Tracy jumped up and slid some coasters under the cans.

"More like an impending explosion," said Kaitlin dryly.

He laughed again, just as Tracy's mother swept into the room, complete with fresh make-up. "Oh, Terry," she said smoothly. Then with a glance at Tracy, she said, "I can't believe no one told me you were here." She laid her hand possessively on his arm. He just smiled at her as she tugged him deeper into the apartment, chatting at him a "mile a minute," as Gramma would have said.

Tracy lay down on the sofa and stared at the ceiling.

"Do you want to go out or something?" Kaitlin suggested.

"Not really," said Tracy. "I think I'm coming down with something. I don't feel well."

Kaitlin eyed her friend. She pulled her science textbook out of her backpack and read potentially pertinent facts aloud. She figured it might help Tracy with the upcoming test as well, although Tracy's only comments about the behaviour of arachnids was an occasional "Eww" and "That's disgusting."

Tracy's energy level hadn't picked up by the end of the chapter. Kaitlin sighed and started reading ahead on amphibians, but silently, just to pass the time. She looked at her watch and wondered what time Mrs. Leeland planned to drive her home. She thought about calling Jane, but she didn't want to offend Tracy either.

Terry came back out into the living room, carrying some tools that had apparently been stashed in the depths of the apartment. "She hid them on me again," he remarked to Tracy.

"She does that," the girl answered, without shifting her gaze from the ceiling.

Kaitlin watched through the window as Terry went back outside and started loosening and tightening things on his bike with a wrench. With a backwards glance at the immobile Tracy, she slipped out the door and sat on the step.

"Hey, there," he said, smiling up at her.

"How old are you?" she asked suddenly.

"Eh?" he grunted, struggling with a tight bolt.

"You look like a teenager," she told him bluntly. "Are you?"

"No way," he returned in mock indignation. "I'm twenty-one. How old are you?"

"Twelve," she answered, lifting her chin.

"Drat," he answered with a wink. "I'll have a long time to wait, I guess."

Kaitlin felt herself blushing.

He laughed and retightened the bolt. "It's nice of Tracy and her mom to let me use their driveway. There's not really any good spot to work on my bike at my apartment building."

"You're not old enough to be Tracy's father, you know."

He looked blank. He sat up suddenly and shook his curly hair out of his eyes. "I'd certainly hope not," he said. "Besides, Tracy already has a father."

Kaitlin hummed softly, considering him. "Well," she continued, lamely, "just so long as you know that."

Terry wiped his palms on his jeans and sat down beside Kaitlin on the step. "I get it. Tracy's mom and I are just friends. She's got a lot of stuff to work out and needs a friend."

"Hmm," Kaitlin said noncommittally. "How did you meet Mrs. Leeland?"

"She's taking a couple of courses at the university, and she's in one of my classes."

"What class?"

"Philosophy—that's my major," he grunted, applying his weight to loosen a bolt.

"Do you want to be a philosopher?"

"You mean, when I grow up?" he teased.

She made a face. "I meant, when you graduate."

"Sure, if anyone wants to hire a philosopher!" He smiled at her. "One sec." He dashed inside and returned with two cans in hand. "Have some root beer," he said. "It's good for you."

"It is not," protested Kaitlin while accepting the proffered pop. She sipped it while he gulped his down.

"I still think you look like a teenager."

He laughed. "I still think you're cute."

She blushed again and scowled at him.

The door creaked open, and Tracy peeked out. "Do you want to take Fred for a walk?" she asked Kaitlin.

"Sure."

Tracy walked carefully down the steps, dangling the tiny dog from its short leash. She slipped her arm through Kaitlin's companionably. "Come on, then."

Terry grinned at the sight of the toy dog hanging from its leash, but he refrained from making any comments. "Tracy," he said, as the girls were walking down the driveway.

She turned and looked at him briefly. "Yes?"

"Have you guys had any lunch?" he tilted his head at the two girls.

Kaitlin interjected. "No, and I'm starving!"

"I'll pick up a pizza. What kind?"

"Hawaiian," both girls responded in unison. They looked at each other and giggled, continuing down the driveway. Kaitlin turned back to see the blonde head rebent over the chrome of his motorcycle. She shouted back at him: "And root beer!"

He laughed and waved in acknowledgement.

"Do you think he's cute?" Tracy asked Kaitlin as soon as they were immediately out of earshot.

Kaitlin eyed her friend warily. "I guess so, for his age. Do you?"

Tracy smiled. "He's gorgeous. But I have to hate him on principle. Like you have to hate Jane."

Kaitlin was unsure of how to respond. Finally, she

blurted out: "I don't think he wants to marry your mom. He said they were just friends."

Tracy made a face and kicked at a leaf. The girls continued their stroll, taking turns walking Fred.

A few minutes later, Terry thundered up beside them on his motorcycle, looking frightening in his black motorcycle gear. He lifted his visor and revved his engine loudly. "Doesn't that sound better?" he asked Kaitlin. She stared at him uncertainly.

He laughed and tilted his head towards the pizza-box strapped to the back of his bike. "Dinner's ready, race you home." He zoomed down the road.

Kaitlin and Tracy eyed each other, then cried, "Run!" Tracy hit the steps first by a second or so, but Kaitlin claimed she was hampered by Fred, who couldn't keep up.

Terry was dishing pizza slices onto plates at the small table. Mrs. Leeland was sitting there, eating half a slice. Kaitlin eyed Mrs. Leeland thoughtfully. "Mrs. Leeland," she said sweetly, "how old are you?"

The woman nearly choked on her pizza. She narrowed her eyes at Kaitlin. "Really. That's not a polite question to ask a woman."

Kaitlin opened her eyes wide in assumed innocence. "It's not? Oh, I'm sorry, I didn't know. I just wondered if you were the same age as my dad, because Tracy and I are the same age."

Mrs. Leeland opened her mouth, but Kaitlin quickly interjected. "My dad's thirty-six," she supplied, smiling.

Mrs. Leeland's eyes narrowed further.

"What a young man your father is, Kaitlin," Terry supplied smoothly.

Mrs. Leeland closed her mouth and picked up her knife and fork. She started cutting her pizza into tiny pieces.

After lunch, Mrs. Leeland retreated into her bedroom to reapply her makeup. She reappeared with a purse tucked under her arm. "Well, I'm off to my yoga class," she said, with a little wave to the girls. "Will you come over for dinner?" she asked Terry.

"Sure," he agreed, but glanced at the girls. "How is Kaitlin getting home?"

Mrs. Leeland frowned slightly, as if reminded of an inconvenience. "I can't be late for my class."

Kaitlin frowned too. She stiffened her back. "I'll call my dad."

"Where do you live?" Terry asked. "I can take you home. No problem."

"What a darling you are," said Mrs. Leeland gratefully.

Kaitlin and Tracy both grimaced.

"You're going to ride on Terry's motorcycle!" Tracy whispered.

Kaitlin pretended it was no big deal as Terry went outside and fastened his saddlebag to his bike. "Will that jacket be warm enough?" he asked. "You can borrow mine if you want."

Kaitlin blushed, and Tracy laughed.

"Oh, no, I'll be fine," she answered, as Terry put his spare helmet on her head and fastened the strap under her chin. He tapped the top of the helmet lightly. "Have you been on many bikes?"

"Only mountain bikes."

"Wonderful. You'll have to tell me how you like

this!" He straddled the bike and tilted his head at her. "Well, get on. I'll see you later, Tracy," he said with a wave. Kaitlin climbed on awkwardly.

He called back. "You'll probably want to hold onto me."

Kaitlin, feeling very uncomfortable, put her hands lightly on his back. The bike moved suddenly with a jerk. Kaitlin gasped and grabbed on more tightly. She wanted to wave good-bye to Tracy, but the bike sped out of the driveway so quickly that Kaitlin was afraid to let go. The wind felt very hard against her cheeks, and her whole jacket was ballooning full of air. At a stop sign, Terry turned and yelled over the roar of the engine, "Are you okay back there?"

Kaitlin nodded her big helmet-head and screamed back, "Yes, fine!" He leaned to the side as he went around a corner. She didn't know if she was relieved or disappointed when the motorcycle turned into her yard, spinning up gravel. She pulled the helmet off and handed it back to him. Her head felt lighter, happy to be out of its container.

"Did you like that?"

"Um," said Kaitlin, "I think so."

"I'll take that as unabashed enthusiasm for motorcycles. When you're older, you should get one." He grinned at her, then gazed up at the house. "Are you okay here?" he asked. "Do you want to make sure someone's home?"

Kaitlin shook her head. "I've got a key."

He nodded, pulled his glove off and extended his hand to Kaitlin. "It was very nice to meet you. I'm so glad you like root beer."

She laughed and shook her head at him. He started up the motorcycle and zoomed out of the driveway, turning once to wave at her. Kaitlin glanced towards the Draysons' and saw Michael standing there, open-mouthed, for once apparently at a loss for words.

She smiled again, tossed her hair and strolled cheerily inside.

Ten

Kaitlin stared in the mirror at Katerina. She pulled her hair away from her face and assumed her haughtiest expression, wondering what she looked like to a twenty-one-year-old. "Like a kid," Katerina scoffed back.

A door slammed outside, and she glanced out her bedroom window. Anna was spinning around in a circle on the front lawn. When she got too dizzy, she'd collapse to the ground, then she'd get back to her feet and start spinning all over again.

Kaitlin's father and Jane were bringing in the groceries. The loud banging of cupboards meant her dad was putting the food away. There was a light knock on her door. She affixed her best scowl in place. "Come in," she said, in as unfriendly a tone as possible.

The knob turned, and Jane peered in the room. "Hi, there. We weren't sure you were home. How was the visit?"

Kaitlin shrugged. "It was okay."

Jane hesitated for a second or two. "May I come in for a moment, Kaitlin?"

Kaitlin shrugged noncommittally. "Whatever."

Jane locked the door behind her, much to Kaitlin's surprise. She was carrying a large bag. She set it on the bed and sat down beside Kaitlin.

The locked door quickly proved effective, as Anna was soon rattling the handle. "Mommy! Mommy!" the little girl screamed. "I want in! Mommy!"

Jane raised her voice slightly to be heard over the din. "I'm busy, dear. Go play with your father!"

Anna protested more loudly. Kaitlin heard her dad arrive to skillfully lure the little girl away. There seemed to be a mention of chocolate in the kitchen, and then all grew silent.

Jane cleared her throat. "Okay, Kaitlin. I realize you're growing up very quickly, and a lot of changes are happening to your body."

Kaitlin's eyes flew open in alarm. It had been way too embarrassing last spring when Jane had painstakingly explained puberty. "We're not going to have the *talk* again, are we? I didn't forget anything." She gestured frantically to the bookshelf. "I read the book you gave me."

"No, no," said Jane quickly. "But you know I'm available if you ever think of a question or want to talk about anything."

Kaitlin made a face.

"I don't mean to upset you, but I thought I'd pick up a few things for you, in case you want or need them at some point." She paused. "I remember when I was a kid, having to ask for this stuff. I just want everything to be comfortable for you."

Kaitlin blinked at her, not feeling particularly comfortable at all. "What's in the bag?" she asked, trying to sound nonchalant.

Jane smiled and in one fell swoop dumped the bag's

contents on the bedcover.

Kaitlin eyed the assortment. She spied the bulky package marked "sanitary napkins" immediately. "I don't need those," she protested, frowning.

"You will sometime, probably soon. You might as well be prepared."

"I'm not a Boy Scout," Kaitlin interjected. But she unlocked her cabinet and shoved the package inside. She locked the door again.

"Put a couple in your locker at school," Jane suggested.

Fingering through the rest of the merchandise, Kaitlin didn't answer. There was a razor and some shaving cream. She looked at Jane again. "What's this for? Do you think I'm hairy?"

"Not at all. I just wanted you to have this, in case you ever need it. In case you want to shave something or other at some point."

Kaitlin raised an eyebrow at her. "Like the hair off my head?"

Jane's cool demeanour didn't change at all. "Perhaps. I'd recommend discussing that with your father first. He might have something to say about it."

Kaitlin giggled in spite of herself. "I bet he would." She turned over a couple more packages. "Oh," she mumbled, discovering a bra wrapped in plastic. She felt uncomfortable again. "I don't need this," she said again, automatically. She glanced quickly at Jane. "Do I?" She almost whispered it.

Jane just smiled back at her. "You certainly don't have to wear it, Kaitlin. I know some of your classmates probably have bras now. It's totally up to you."

She picked up a tube of lipstick and raised a curious eyebrow at Jane, who, surprisingly, looked a bit sheepish. "Okay, I got a bit carried away." She handed Kaitlin a small make-up compact. "I wanted to throw in some more fun growing-up stuff." She shrugged as Kaitlin reached for the last item on the bed. "Okay, I got quite a bit carried away."

"What is it?" Kaitlin asked curiously, turning the thing over in her hand.

Jane blushed slightly. "I took it out of a bin marked 'eyelash curlers.'"

Kaitlin was quite astonished. She looked at Jane's eyes. "Do you use an eyelash-curler?" she asked.

Jane shook her head. "No, I never have. I'm sorry. It was an impulse buy. You don't have to keep it. Here, give it to me, and I'll take it away."

"No!" Kaitlin protested. She gripped the strange metal object tightly. "I want it." She was startled at her own vehemence and peered more closely at the unusual device.

Jane stood up from the bed. "Well, that's it. I just wanted to give you that stuff in private." She walked over to the door, unlocked it and pulled it open.

"Jane," Kaitlin called before she realized what she was doing. Jane turned, looking back at her, questioningly.

Swallowing, Kaitlin glanced at the rug before turning her eyes back to Jane. "Thank you," she whispered softly. Of course, she regretted the words as soon as she'd spoken them.

Jane looked a bit surprised, but she nodded briskly. "You're welcome, Kaitlin." She closed the door gently behind her.

Eleven

A ll right, class," said Ms. Manon, pacing across the front of the classroom, decorated liberally with the students' essays and dubious artwork.

"I know this is only Grade Seven. You still have a lot of time to decide what you want to do with your lives." She folded her arms and contemplated her students. "But it won't hurt to start thinking about your futures now. For today's assignment, I'd like you to start by compiling a short list of job occupations that interest you."

She let her intense gaze travel from student to student. "I don't want anybody to feel constrained by gender or any other kind of stereotype, either. I want you to think about what would genuinely be interesting to you, and come up with a short list." She picked up a few papers from the top of her desk and slipped out of the room.

Kaitlin frowned at her blank paper. Ms. Manon had taught a whole class recently just on the topic of stereotypes. She told the kids that they should never feel they needed to act a specific way, or choose a type of job, just because they were male or female, or rich or poor, or because of their race. They'd talked about all kinds of stereotypes, even silly things, like that smart kids wear glasses, all tall kids excel at basketball, and all Canadians are good at hockey.

Ms. Manon said it was a stereotype to say that girls are afraid of insects. Kaitlin, however, was afraid of certain bugs, especially spiders. But then again, so was Chuck, although he wouldn't admit it.

Kaitlin carefully wrote "Microbiologist" at the top of her list.

Glenn leaned over and eyed her page. "Ooh, microbiologist," he grinned. "I'm impressed. And, Winter?" he asked. "Can you top that?" He shifted to see what Winter had written, and laughed. "I think she's got you, Kaitlin, with 'neurosurgeon.'"

Winter smiled. She scrawled "astronaut" for her second choice.

"I can't think of anything non-stereotypical," Chuck complained irritably.

"Try 'nurse,'" Glenn suggested.

"Get outta here," Chuck mumbled uncertainly.

"I want to be a nurse," protested Audrey, at the back of the class. "Is that too stereotypical?" The pale girl sounded distressed.

"If that's what you want to be, it's fine for your list," Kaitlin said.

"Just don't expect a pat on the head," Glenn interjected. "But if a guy writes that on his list, she'll love it."

Chuck didn't answer, but he wrote something down. Glenn scratched a word on his own paper and held it out to Kaitlin. She squinted at the messy writing. He'd written "homemaker" at the top of his list.

Kaitlin giggled. "Big aspirations."

Glenn nodded, grinning widely. "Hey, I'm willing to let a woman support me." He cocked his head thoughtfully. "Who makes more money, a microbiologist or a neurosurgeon?"

There was a snort from Winter's direction.

Then Chuck spoke again. "Hey, Kaitlin's wearing a bra!"

The whole class turned to look at her. Kaitlin wanted to hide under her desk. Tracy frowned, and Kaitlin wondered briefly if Tracy's mother would think to buy her one. Out of the corner of her eye, she saw Glenn appraise her, and she blushed deeply. But he quickly snatched up a ruler from the top of his desk and whacked Chuck with it, not gently. "You charmer," Glenn chided.

Chuck was blushing profusely. "Sorry, I just noticed …sorry…" he mumbled, his voice trailing off.

"You never noticed that I wear a bra," Audrey protested.

Chuck's face turned a darker red. "Uh, uh…"

Turning around in her desk, Winter saw Kaitlin's stricken expression. "Oh, Kaitlin," she exclaimed brightly. "You've just got to come shopping with me." She slipped a thumb under the neckline of her yellow top to pull out a bright orange bra strap. "Fluorescent! Can you imagine?" She let the strap snap back into place.

Kaitlin smiled gratefully.

Chuck dropped his face against the top of his desk and moaned.

*　　*　　*

Tossing her books haphazardly into the bottom of her locker, Kaitlin tapped her foot, waiting impatiently for Tracy to carefully stack her colour-coded notebooks.

"Here, hold Fred for me," said Tracy.

Sighing, Kaitlin shoved the dog under one arm. "Fred doesn't like to be held like that," Tracy said.

Winter was adjusting her carefully bunched yellow socks over her ankles on top of her bright orange tights. "Do you want to hold this dog?" Kaitlin asked hopefully.

Winter gave a short, loud laugh. "Don't even think about it."

They slipped into the girls' washroom, and Kaitlin brought out her newly acquired eyelash-curler. She nonchalantly started curling her eyelashes, glancing out of the corner of her eye as Tracy shrieked. "Where did you get that? Can I try?"

Kaitlin shrugged. "Sure, if you want. Jane bought it for me." She blinked, thinking the curled lashes felt a bit stiff on her eyelids.

"Wow," said Tracy. "You're so lucky. I've always wanted one of those."

Winter leaned against the mirror and grinned at them both. "Beware of stepmothers bearing eyelash curlers," she teased. Kaitlin made a face. But even the ever-cool Winter took a turn with the curler after Tracy had finished.

"Do you think anyone will notice?" Tracy asked, batting her lashes towards the mirror.

"I doubt it," Winter murmured. "But they'll notice

this." She took a small container out of her pocket, and pasted a tiny orange star just under the corner of one eye, above her cheekbone.

"Wow," said Tracy. "Do you have an extra that I can wear?"

Winter smiled serenely at her. "Yes, but not today, dear. A trendsetter has to go out on her own, before the crowd follows."

Kaitlin snorted. "You're such a…" she paused, thinking of a properly impressive word, "such an *exhibitionist!* I'm not going to paste a star on my face," she added firmly.

"You'll be unique then, when everyone else is wearing one." Winter said unabashedly. Suddenly, she clapped her hands together. "So. Isn't anyone else curious to see whether Andrew's got any email?"

Kaitlin shrieked and grabbed Tracy's hand. "Yes! Come on! Your eyelashes look great." The girls giggled as they ran out into the hall.

They literally collided with a group of Grade Eight boys who were walking past. The guys seemed to find the resulting traffic jam quite amusing. "Careful there," said Michael, grasping Kaitlin's arm to steady her.

"You girls seem to be in a hurry," commented Brad, shoulder-to-shoulder with Michael, standing in Kaitlin's path. "Where are you off to?"

"To make trouble, no doubt," drawled Michael.

She pulled herself free and raised her head, deciding not to dignify the boys' questions with a response. Michael shook his head but moved aside to let her by.

"Nice star," Brad commented, a bit snidely.

Winter smiled her dangerous smile. "Well, Brad," she said in a whisper, leaning in towards him, "I was hoping you would think so." She slipped a hand under Kaitlin's and Tracy's respective elbows, guiding them away from the scene. "I think we were heading this way, girls," she suggested.

Glancing backwards over her shoulder, Kaitlin saw Brad gaping at Winter. Then her gaze fell on Michael's infuriating grin. Her head snapped back around. "Right," she said firmly, "to the computer lab."

The girls shouted with delight to find an email to Andrew from Shelley. Tracy read it aloud.

Dear Andrew:

I was surprised but flattered to get your email that said you've noticed me.

In answer to your questions, I'm in Grade Eight, and I am 13 years old. I am a cheerleader and like cheerleading very much. I'm especially good at cartwheeling, but I can shout very loudly, which is also a valuable skill.

You said you're in Grade 10. How old are you? Do you get to this part of town much? Do you usually write to girls you don't know?

But you can write more if you want.

Shelley

p.s. I wonder what you look like.

Kaitlin danced about. So did Tracy. Even Winter was laughing.

"Well, well," said Glenn at the door, followed by a still-sheepish Chuck. "Have we had some success?" He tilted his head towards the screen inquiringly.

Before Kaitlin could open her mouth to protest, Tracy was encouraging the boys to read the letter.

"How about that," said Glenn, poking Chuck lightly. "All it took was a sappy letter to get an email from Shelley. So, Kaitlin, the ball's back in your court. Now what?"

"On with the game, of course." She typed carefully:

Dear Shelley:
I'm so glad you wrote back.
I'm 12 years old…

"He's twelve in Grade Ten!" Chuck interjected. "Smart kid."

"But Andrew *is* twelve," Tracy protested, her eyebrows drawn tight together. "I guess he must have skipped some grades."

Kaitlin shook her head. "Shelley won't be interested in a twelve-year-old. Andrew will have to lie about his age."

"Not the honest Andrew…" Winter said, mock-scandalized.

Kaitlin ignored her and back-spaced:

I'm 15 years old. Cross-my-heart you are the first girl I've ever emailed.
Sometimes I do get across town, and hope maybe to meet you one day soon, if that's not too bold.
What do I look like? Well, I have long blonde hair…

"I thought Andrew had dark hair," Winter interrupted, sounding curious.

Tracy giggled and poked Kaitlin lightly. "Umm..." Kaitlin faltered.

"It's blonde under fluorescent light," Tracy explained calmly, ignoring Winter's skeptical gaze.

...and dark blue eyes,

Kaitlin wrote.

"Weren't they green?" Winter asked blandly. Tracy opened her mouth to reply, but Winter waved her hand. "Not under fluorescent lights, I know..."

"Curly blonde hair," said Tracy, prodding Kaitlin. The two girls shared a secret smile.

I have long curly blonde hair and dark blue eyes.

It's hard for me to know, but some girls in my class have said I'm cute.

Did I mention that I'm learning to drive? I want to get my licence as soon as I turn 16.

Maybe some day soon I'll get to see your cartwheels.

Andrew.

Chuck and Glenn laughed loudly, as if it were the funniest thing they'd ever read.

Winter just shook her head. She gazed at Kaitlin curiously. "Trouble was right," she murmured.

Twelve

Pushing the door open, Winter stepped over the threshold of her house. "Come on in," she gestured to Kaitlin, seemingly oblivious to the din inside. Someone was pounding on the piano. There were sounds of footsteps running across floorboards, and there was loud talking, shrieking and laughing.

Cautiously, Kaitlin followed her friend down the hallway. The exuberance of Winter's family was somewhat alarming. Sure enough, Winter's mother peered around the corner and quickly enveloped Kaitlin in her substantial bear-hug. "Kaitlin! It's been way too long! How have you been, dear girl?"

Kaitlin tentatively hugged her back. "I'm fine, Mrs. Carter-Jones. How are you?"

Winter's mom released her. "Oh, you're such a sweetie. I'm very well, thank you for asking. Come in, come in. We just finished a batch of chocolate-chip cookies. Come have a taste, dear." She beamed at Kaitlin and bustled into the kitchen.

Winter grinned. "You okay? I know you're not much into public displays of affection."

Kaitlin scowled and Winter laughed, grabbing her

arm and pulling her into the kitchen. Winter's father was reading a newspaper at the table and sampling one of the cookies. He pushed his eyeglasses up past his forehead and eyed Kaitlin with delight. "Well, look who it is!" he exclaimed. "It's the very bright Kaitlin who forces Winter to study."

"Oh, shush you," interceded his wife. "Don't discourage them. Healthy competition is a good thing. And think of the great study skills they're learning."

Sighing in false exasperation, Winter grabbed two cookies and handed one to Kaitlin.

Winter winced as the unseen pianist hit a wrong note, and she led Kaitlin into the dining room, where her older sister Ruth was practising. "Ow!" yelled Winter. "Ouch! Ow!" She covered her ears in mock agony. "Stop, please, you're killing me."

The tall girl turned around and made a face at Winter. "Thanks for the encouragement, eh? Hey, Kaitlin," she smiled. "I finally managed to teach Winter the full rendition of 'Chopsticks'. Wanna hear?"

"Sure," Kaitlin nodded, settling down on the sofa.

Flexing her hands as if she were a virtuoso pianist, Winter sat down on the piano bench. She carefully plodded out the melody while Ruth embellished the piece with fancy improvisation on her half of the piano.

Kaitlin applauded with due enthusiasm when they finished. Winter jumped up and bowed deeply, but her older sister just smiled and gave a slight nod to acknowledge the tribute.

"Of course," said Ruth. "Winter's the singer in the family."

Winter looked embarrassed and leaned over to poke her sister. Ruth just laughed. "Wouldn't you like to hear Winter sing?"

"Umm, sure," said Kaitlin. She raised an eyebrow questioningly.

Winter grimaced. "Oh, fine." She started singing an Irish ballad that Kaitlin had never heard before.

Kaitlin was astonished. Her friend's voice reverberated rich and resonant throughout the house. The background sound quieted as Winter's parents slipped in behind Kaitlin. Winter's brother Felix ducked through the door from the living room, bouncing their small sister Sara on his shoulders. When Winter came to the chorus again, Kaitlin stared in surprise as the entire family joined in, singing heartily. When the song came to a close, Winter collapsed on the sofa beside Kaitlin.

"Weird, huh?"

"Definitely."

Winter laughed and hit her friend with a sofa cushion.

"Seriously. I thought I was on the set of some sort of TV show."

"Oh, well," shrugged Winter, "I feel like that all the time."

Felix snorted and dumped Sara without ceremony into an armchair. "Hey, brat," he murmured to Winter.

"Hey, repugnant guttersnipe," she replied without pausing.

"Now, children," interceded Mrs. Carter-Jones. "Be nice, please."

The kids grinned at each other as their mother headed back into the kitchen. "Oh, Kaitlin. We're having chicken for dinner. What's your favourite vegetable? Corn, carrots or beans?"

"Corn, please."

"Whew," said Felix, nodding to Kaitlin as he followed his parents into the kitchen. "Good choice, kid."

Ruth laughed as she gathered up her music. "Now he's your friend for life." The tall girl stood up and slipped into the hall.

"Felix gave me a ride on his shoulders," Sara giggled, lying across the chair exactly as she'd been dropped. "Will you carry me too?" she asked Winter.

"No way," Winter replied cheerfully. "You weigh a ton."

Kaitlin eyed Sara thoughtfully. She was about Anna's age and was dressed in a pretty yellow dress with multicoloured ribbons adorning the many braids in her short dark hair. She ran over to the couch and threw herself onto Winter's lap.

Groaning dramatically, Winter lifted her sister into a sitting position on her knee.

Kaitlin watched them pensively for a moment, thinking how different this family was from her own household. And it was definitely a far cry from Tracy's family. She felt a touch on her arm from Winter's little sister.

"Hi, Sara."

Sara snuggled close. "Can I ride on your shoulders?" she asked.

Kaitlin shook her head apologetically. "I don't think so."

Sara leaned closer to Kaitlin, her expression bright and eager. "Can I sit on your knee, then?"

Hesitating briefly, Kaitlin glanced at Winter's smiling eyes and then back at the small girl. "I guess so," she answered gruffly.

The small, warm, squirming bundle threw itself onto Kaitlin's lap. Winter chuckled in private amusement. Kaitlin smiled at her over Sara's delighted head.

*   *   *

Despite a slight chill in the air, Kaitlin opened her window, allowing a cool breeze to waft into her bedroom. She lay prone on her bed, staring at the ceiling. The smaller animals swayed slightly on their strings, as if appreciative of the wind's visit. Kaitlin propped up her pillow and folded her arms, contemplating the gentle movements of the pink rabbit. There was a light tap on the door. "Katie?" her father's voice inquired tentatively.

"It's not locked!" Kaitlin sat up on her bed, her arms casually hugging her knees. "Hi, Dad."

"Hi, there, Katie." He had some paper in his hand but kept it almost hidden behind him as he closed the door and gazed gently at her. His expression looked troubled. Kaitlin felt a slight ripple of alarm in her stomach as her father looked at her in that disquieting manner. "How are you?" he asked finally.

"Okay," she replied quickly, tilting her head at him. "How are you?"

"I'm okay too." And still he watched her in that odd way.

"Are you sure, Dad?" she asked.

"Sure, yes. Everything's fine."

But she still felt uncertain, especially when her father cleared his throat as if he had something important to say. And when he reached out and placed his big hand over hers, Kaitlin's mind raced, trying to imagine what dreaded news he might be about to impart. She tensed. "What's wrong, Dad?"

He shook his head slightly and smiled as if to reassure her. "Oh, dear, nothing's wrong. It's just that I have something to give you, and I'm not sure if it's a good idea, or if this is the right time. She told me I'd know when it was the right time, and I think it is…but I'm not sure."

Kaitlin's brows drew tightly together. "Who told you?" she asked.

Dad sighed deeply. "Sweetie," he said, "your mother wrote you a letter when she was sick and asked me to give it to you when you were older."

"My mother wrote me a letter?" Kaitlin repeated uncertainly.

He patted her hand once, looking out into space as he spoke. "I know how hard it's been for you all these years since she died. I've been hoping you've been feeling a bit better lately." He sighed. "I don't want to upset you, but you're getting older, and you have the right to the letter your mother wrote to you."

Kaitlin stared at him in astonishment. Her heart was beating very fast, and she could feel a painful pricking under her eyelids.

"I can put the letter away until you want it," he offered in an almost pleading tone.

Kaitlin swallowed hard. "I want it now," she said flatly. She lifted her gaze to meet her father's until he nodded.

"I thought you'd say that." He gave her a sad smile as he handed her the thin ivory envelope. It was sealed. A simple "Kaitlin" was written in her mother's neat hand across the front.

"Have you read it?" she asked quietly.

"Your mom showed it to me after she wrote it, before she sealed the envelope. A lot was going on at the time, so I don't remember the letter very well. I don't think I wanted to dwell on it. I didn't want to believe she would actually be leaving us." He gave a small sigh. His eyes were moist as he gazed as his daughter.

"Mom...knew...she knew she was dying?" she whispered.

Nodding, he lifted himself slowly off the bed, leaning over to give her a gentle hug. "I'll leave you alone now. I'll be around if you want to talk. Whenever you want to talk, I'm here, okay?"

Kaitlin held herself stiffly, protecting the fragile envelope. "I know, Dad." She gazed at her name, in her mother's handwriting.

"It's a bit chilly in here," he commented. "Do you want me to shut the window?"

"Okay." She lightly touched her name, thinking of her mother's pen lingering over those letters. She heard the sound of the window closing. Her father hesitated a moment longer before letting himself out of the room and shutting the door quietly behind him.

She got up and locked the door. Her whole body was

trembling. She pressed a fingernail under the edge of the envelope, but it was very well pasted down. She found a slightly loosened spot and carefully worked the paper apart, anxious not to rip the envelope. Ever so slowly, she slipped the paper out of the envelope and unfolded it. The writing was very even, as if her mother had very carefully planned each word.

Kaitlin gently spread out the page and read the letter.

To my darling daughter, Kaitlin

Hello sweetheart. I am writing this, knowing it will be several years before you read these words. Today, as you play on the floor beside my bed, I look at your sweet little face and your tousled hair and know you're too young to understand what's happening to me. That's why I'm going to ask your father to hold this letter until you are older, my dearest.

When the doctors first told me I had cancer, and when it became obvious that I would not recover, I felt devastated. I prayed to God and asked him: "Why me? I have a very small child and a husband who both need me very much."

But although it sounds incredible, I've come to feel a surprising peace in my heart. I realize: Why not me? I've had the chance to be married to an absolutely wonderful man, and I've borne a delightful lovely child, and you both love me so much. I've had the best possible life, so why not me?

Kaitlin, I'm confident of the life to come after death. I have faith that I will see you again when the time is right.

My daughter, you are my pride and my joy. I know you

will do great things with your life. I already know you are bright and strong-willed. I have the utmost confidence that you will grow to be a caring loving woman with strength and purpose. Know that your mother has very high expectations for you, dear girl.

Please take care of your father. I know he will be lonely.

I honestly hope that your dad will find another woman to love, and am trusting she will be someone kind and decent who will take very good care of my precious family. That's what I want.

And some day, I hope you will find a good, caring man to marry, like I did. Choose carefully. Find someone loving and brave and absolutely special, a man who will love you wholeheartedly your entire life through.

Now you have climbed up on the bed beside me here as I write. You want to snuggle, so I think that must be a sign I've written enough.

I can't tell you how sorry I am that I won't get to see you grow up. But I know I will see you some day in Heaven, and then you can tell me about every single detail that I've missed.

I love you so very much.

Mom

Kaitlin read the letter again, tears streaming down her face.

She sank to the floor, pressing her face into her arms on the side of the bed, and sobbed.

*   *   *

Later, she sat on the edge of her windowsill and watched as the creamy pinks and yellows of the setting sun blended with the blue-grey sky of the late afternoon, melting into the horizon. She heard the faint ringing of the telephone in the hall.

A few moments later, there was a light tap on her door. Kaitlin crossed the room and turned the knob.

"It's Tracy, on the phone," said Jane softly, her gaze quickly taking in Kaitlin's tear-stained face. "Do you want to take it?"

Kaitlin swallowed.

"Why don't I tell her you'll call her back later?"

With a soft sniff, Kaitlin nodded. She watched as Jane picked up the receiver again and spoke briefly with Tracy, before hanging up the phone. "She says she's on her way to her mother's for the night, but she'll see you at school tomorrow."

"Okay." Kaitlin's voice broke slightly in the middle of the word.

Jane's brow was creased in an expression of concern. "Are you all right, Kaitlin?" she asked, simply.

Kaitlin nodded wordlessly. She stared into Jane's worried face. "My mother wrote me a letter," she blurted out suddenly, and to her embarrassment, the tears streamed anew.

Jane hesitated only a second. She stepped forward and wrapped Kaitlin in a very tight hug. "Oh, sweetie," she said, as Kaitlin sobbed full-force against her shoulder. Jane smoothed her hair as if she were just a little child. It seemed a very long time before Kaitlin could stop crying. She moved awkwardly away from

Jane, wiping at her face with the back of her hand. Jane murmured something and slipped into the hall, just to return a moment later with a box of tissues.

Kaitlin sniffed and wiped at her face. "Thanks," she whispered quietly. Then without thinking it through, she offered: "Do you want to read the letter?"

Jane stared at her. "Only if you want me to read it," she said finally.

Carefully smoothing the page, Kaitlin handed the paper to Jane, who silently started to read.

It seemed like Jane took a very long time to read the letter. Finally, she lifted her head. There were unshed tears sparkling in her eyes. "Oh, Kaitlin," she said. "It's so sad, but so special too. She loved you and your dad so much."

"I know," Kaitlin whispered.

Reaching out, Jane lightly brushed her fingertips against Kaitlin's cheek, wiping away a stray tear. Oddly, Kaitlin still didn't pull away. For a long moment, they just looked at each other. Jane gave a soft sigh, her gaze then travelling past Kaitlin to the window. "Do you know what I'm going to do? I think I'll make some hot chocolate and go sit on the porch for a while, and look at the sky. Would you like to join me?" Jane asked.

Kaitlin hesitated only a second. "Okay. I'll be right down." Slipping down the stairs, she peeked into the living room, where her father and Anna were curled up on the chesterfield, both engrossed in a *Sesame Street* rerun. Outside, she sat down on the porch swing. When Jane came out with the steaming hot chocolate, Kaitlin moved to one side so Jane could sit beside her.

They didn't say anything, just quietly rocked and watched the sunset finally evaporate into the evening sky.

They didn't notice when the boy next door peered through the tall hedge—just to watch Kaitlin as she sipped chocolate with none other than Jane.

Thirteen

She thinks he sounds very mature!" gasped Tracy, before collapsing in a fit of giggles. The girls were once again huddled around a computer, delighted with the progress of the electronic relationship between Shelley and Andrew.

The tone of the correspondence had even blossomed into light flirtation. Shelley had, to her credit, mentioned the fact that she had a boyfriend, but yet she seemed to maintain a high level of interest in her new online pen pal.

"Of course Andrew sounds mature," scoffed Kaitlin mercilessly. "Shelley's easily impressed."

"Not like you, hmm?" Winter laughed. "Nothing impresses you!"

Kaitlin grinned. "That's right."

"What's this?" Glenn protested. "Kaitlin's never impressed? I'll have to try harder then."

Winter snorted. Kaitlin blushed, despite her best attempt to hide it. She pointedly ignored Glenn, turning her attention back to the last email. At first, she'd been delighted when Shelley had emailed over her school photo, because it was a sign that the plan was working.

But then, to Kaitlin's horror, Shelley had just asked for a picture of Andrew.

Tracy and Kaitlin stared at each other in despair.

Glenn and Chuck were more interested in trying to wrest the keyboard from Winter's grasp to print off some copies of Shelley's smiling face. Winter prevailed, leaving the guys rubbing their shins.

In her alarm, Tracy shrieked and danced nervously about. "We're trapped! What will we do? What will we do!"

Kaitlin grabbed her friend's arm. "Don't worry," she whispered. "I have an idea." She narrowed her eyes at Tracy. "But I'm going to need your help." She took a deep breath. "I need you to ask your mom's friend Terry for a photo of himself when he was a bit younger."

Tracy's eyes flew wide open in understanding. "Ooh," she murmured thoughtfully. "I'll have to tell him it's for you, though. I don't want him to think it's me who wants the photo."

Kaitlin shrugged impatiently. "Tell him whatever you want." She stepped back over to Winter and requested: "*Relinquish* that, please," as she took over the keyboard to type something from Andrew to Shelley about needing a bit of time to get a photo scanned.

Winter grinned. "I give it to you, with *alacrity*, Kaitlin."

Kaitlin rolled her eyes and typed some compliments about Shelley's grey-blue eyes.

*   *   *

Tracy didn't shirk her responsibility. In just two days, she arrived at Kaitlin's house grasping a small package wrapped in brown paper.

"Tracy! Tracy!" shrieked Anna, delightedly clasping the bigger girl around her knees. "What's that? Is it for me?"

Tracy carefully extricated herself, smiling at her. "Sorry Anna—it's for Kaitlin."

Anna pouted prettily. She folded her chubby arms in front of her. "What is it?" she asked petulantly.

Tracy looked disconcerted. "Umm, I don't know."

Anna eyed her suspiciously, reaching one grubby hand towards the package. But Jane intervened, quickly taking her young daughter by that insistent hand. "Let the big girls play by themselves, dear. I've got a treat for you in the kitchen. Come see."

Anna allowed herself to be led off, but threw numerous backward glances over her shoulder at the small package.

In the security of Kaitlin's room, Tracy handed over the paper-covered package. "This is for you," she said, "from Terry."

"Oh," said Kaitlin, trying to sound nonchalant. But without further ado, she tore open the packaging. Inside was a photograph, a can of root beer and a small folded note. She opened the paper to reveal some rather unruly handwriting.

Dear Kaitlin,
Tracy explained a bit about why you want this photo. I'm always happy to help; just try not to get me arrested or

anything like that, okay?

I've included some root beer for you, just because.

Take it easy,

Terry

Kaitlin reread the note, blushing under Tracy's perplexed stare. "Why did he give you pop? I don't get it."

Kaitlin shook her head. "Who knows?" she asked, trying to sound casual.

"Let's drink it," prompted Tracy. But Kaitlin shook her head. "No. If you're thirsty, there's stuff in the fridge downstairs." Emphasizing the point, she opened up her cupboard, and locked both the can of pop and the note inside. It was her first letter from a guy, after all. Tracy giggled.

Kaitlin thought her friend seemed a bit happier lately. Tracy had to do a lot of the cooking and cleaning at her dad's house now, but she seemed to be handling it okay. She'd even borrowed a cookbook from Jane.

"I thought you'd be checking out the photo!" Tracy rebuked, breaking in on Kaitlin's musings.

"Oh, right!" Kaitlin picked it up to examine closely. It was unmistakably Terry, but a few years younger. His face was smoother, and his curly blonde hair was fairly short.

She held the photo out to Tracy, and they both inspected it critically for a moment. "Do you think Shelley will like him?" Tracy asked pensively.

"Uh-huh," answered Kaitlin. "I think so."

146

*   *   *

The next day, Shelley received a photo of Andrew. She wrote back that he was the cutest boy she'd ever seen.

Glenn frowned at that, reading over Kaitlin's shoulder, as always.

"Who is that guy in the photo, anyway?" asked Chuck curiously.

"Well," said Tracy, pausing, "he's a friend of Kaitlin's."

"That right, Kaitlin?" asked Glenn, with a raised eyebrow. "He's your friend?"

Kaitlin blinked at Tracy but gave a quick nod.

"Ah. I thought you didn't much like boys," Glenn drawled.

She lifted her head and met his gaze. "For the most part, they're pretty annoying."

"Kaitlin even rode on his motorcycle," Tracy interjected, eyeing Glenn's expression with interest.

"Ah," said Glenn, sounding amused. "An older man!" But he continued to gaze at Kaitlin, until she looked away.

Fourteen

Grasping her rollerblades tightly against her chest, Kaitlin sat on the school steps with Winter and Tracy. There was a buzz of excitement in the air as the students prepared for the ten-kilometre blade-a-thon organized to raise money for cancer research.

Kaitlin had raised a lot of money in pledges in the neighbourhood. Whenever anyone had hesitated, she'd sighed and reminded them that her mother had died of cancer, and they'd quickly write a large amount on her pledge sheet. It was strange, but Kaitlin almost felt like she was trying to do something for her mother through this blade-a-thon. She'd been practising her blading with Winter for weeks, up and down the neighbourhood streets.

Tracy's efforts were more lacklustre, but oddly, she was the most keyed up as the girls laced up their skates. "So, who are you girls going to blade with?" she asked merrily.

Winter raised an eyebrow. "Other than you two and the rest of the school?"

Tracy tossed her hair impatiently. "Don't you know that this is a great opportunity?"

"What are you talking about?" Kaitlin said.

"Well," said Tracy coyly, "Chuck said he wanted to

blade with me." She leaned back and watched her friends, to judge their reaction to this news. Seeing none, she continued: "I might prefer Glenn, if he didn't have such a crush on you, Kaitlin. Anyhow, that will work out well, because we can each have a boy."

Kaitlin frowned. "Glenn does *not* have a crush on me!"

But Tracy just waved her protestations aside. "The only problem is I don't have a boy for Winter!" She sighed apologetically.

Winter made a sound deep in her throat. "When I'm inclined, I'll be perfectly capable of finding my own...MAN," she retorted. But then an amused expression passed over her face as she glanced upwards. "Why, hello there, Glenn. Been standing there long?"

Kaitlin felt her whole face grow warm, even before Glenn calmly answered. "Actually, yes."

Chuck skated up just then, and she was spared having to look up at Glenn. "Hey, hurry up. We've got to get to the starting line," said Chuck.

Winter smirked mercilessly. "Getting to that starting line sounds good right about now, eh, Kaitlin?"

She pushed herself away from the step. Tracy, it turned out, needed Chuck's help to get to her feet.

Hundreds of kids started the race together, but Kaitlin and her friends quickly passed most of the smaller children. A number of streets had been closed to traffic. The students had to go around the designated path four times to achieve ten kilometres. Many of the younger kids only made it around once or twice though.

At certain intervals, the teachers had set up sound

systems which blared loud music, but the sound would fade out between the blocks, and the sound of rollerblades would take over as they glided along the pavement. Every now and then the sound of muffled thumps and yells signalled that yet another kid had wiped out.

It was a bright sunny day, although the air was cool. The girls had dressed in layers they could take off in case it got too hot. Winter's layers, of course, were mainly fluorescent.

It seemed that Tracy's predictions were true. A significant number of the older kids soon paired up as they took off down the streets. Tracy seemed to have particular difficulty staying on her feet until she grasped onto Chuck for support. Once he was holding her hand, her blading improved greatly, although he didn't seem to notice.

Kaitlin nearly tripped at the sudden sound of Glenn's voice very close to her ear. "So, Kaitlin," he said, "wanna hold my hand?"

Kaitlin blinked at him in alarm. "No!"

He laughed, falling in beside her, matching her pace. "No? Well, let me know if you change your mind."

She glanced over at him, and he was smiling warmly at her. Just then, across the road, she noticed Michael coming around the corner with his gang of friends, including Shelley, who was gripping his arm tightly and seemed a bit unsteady on her skates.

Kaitlin felt the feeling in her stomach get worse as she looked at Michael and Shelley. "Okay," she blurted to Glenn.

"Hmm?" he answered, surprised.

She frowned at him with impatience. "I'll hold your hand."

"Ooh," he murmured, "by all means." He reached out and caught Kaitlin's hand in a firm grip. She almost stumbled.

He steadied her with his grasp. "Okay, Kaitlin. It will be easier if we skate together. See, right foot, left foot—that's right." He smiled encouragingly at her, and she tried to keep to the rhythm.

She looked over towards Michael. Her neighbour raised an eyebrow at her. She jerked her head around again, falling out of rhythm. "You know, Kaitlin," Glenn said, "it works better if you look where you're going. Or," he added, "you could look at me, if you like."

"Don't push it," she muttered, blushing. Glenn laughed loudly.

Winter shook her head in mock despair. "You slowpokes!" She skated briskly across to Michael's group. "Hey, *Brad*," she said, emphasizing his name. "I hear you're a fast blader."

He looked surprised but shrugged at her. "Not bad."

"Huh," said Winter. "You look pretty slow to me. Show me your stuff, boy!" And she took off down the road, her long purple-clad legs streaking into the distance. Kaitlin watched as Brad said something to Michael, then sped after her. Winter merely picked up speed as he approached, and they disappeared into the distance.

Glenn whistled lightly. "She's really something." But he squeezed Kaitlin's hand.

"Yes, she is," Kaitlin echoed.

After a while, her muscles started to ache. But she reminded herself that she was raising some money for cancer research. To her surprise, it almost seemed as if Glenn could read her thoughts. "Are you thinking about your mother?" he asked quietly.

She glanced at him in surprise and answered almost shyly. "Yeah."

They finally pulled up to the finish line, to the applause of the teachers and the younger students who had given up earlier. She noticed Tracy and Chuck were among them. Kaitlin pulled herself out of Glenn's grasp and skated over to Winter. "So who was first?"

Winter and Brad exchanged glances. "She was," he said, with an easy smile. "But she tricked me."

"Oh?" asked Kaitlin questioningly, but no one explained. Winter and Brad just grinned at each other.

Some of the other senior kids were reaching the finish line. Michael dumped a weary Shelley rather unceremoniously onto the grass at the side of the road.

Glenn stared out down the street. "Let's go one more time," he said, looking at Kaitlin.

"Are you crazy?" squeaked Tracy from where she lay on the ground.

"Let's go one more time—for Kaitlin's mom," Glenn said.

Kaitlin felt something warm trembling inside her chest.

Winter wiped her palms on her tights and nodded firmly. "Yes, let's do it. Come on, Kaitlin," she said, touching her lightly on the shoulder. No one paid any attention to Tracy's protestations.

Kaitlin, Winter and Glenn started down the road. Kaitlin was startled a moment later to realize Michael had joined them, followed by Brad and Chuck.

No one said anything at all. They just moved along silently, almost in unison. The only sound came from the rollerblades gliding down the road. Kaitlin ignored her aching muscles. She lifted her head and put all her energy into her legs. She looked at the others who skated with her, in honour of her mother.

In that moment, she felt as though her heart might burst.

*   *   *

There was a marked chill to the air. Kaitlin pulled her jacket up tight against her neck and shivered as she crunched through the fallen leaves in the ancient graveyard. It was late afternoon, and the sky was grey.

"I told the guys to meet us at Andrew's gravestone," whispered Tracy melodramatically. "After all, he brought us together."

Kaitlin scowled. "We're not together."

Her friend squinted back. "I don't know why you're not happy that we have boyfriends."

Kaitlin sighed deeply. "Glenn is *not* my boyfriend," she protested.

But Tracy just shook her head and started collecting some red maple leaves. "The flowers are all dead. I hope Andrew likes leaves."

Tracy carefully stacked a small pile of leaves in front of the gravestone. Kaitlin slowly ran her fingertips over the cool rock, absorbing the feel of the lettering. "I wish we could have known him," she sighed softly.

Tracy nodded. "I bet Andrew was great."

"Hey," called out Chuck cheerfully, from across the graveyard. "Are you girls mooning over old Andrew again?"

Kaitlin frowned, but Tracy smiled brightly.

"Hey, Kaitlin," said Glenn, watching her closely.

"Hi," she answered shortly. She leaned down to arrange the pile of leaves to her satisfaction.

"What a lovely bouquet," he teased. "In fact, I'm jealous."

"Don't worry. I'd put dead leaves on your grave."

Glenn pressed a hand to his heart as if wounded. "Oh, Kaitlin, you're so harsh." But he reached out his hand. "Come walk with me."

Kaitlin glanced over at Tracy, but her friend and Chuck were reading the old headstones and giggling. Kaitlin wondered what was so humorous. She put her hand in Glenn's, and he squeezed it reassuringly as he led her away from them. "I want to get out of the graveyard," he explained. "I know you guys like to hang out here, but I find it a bit creepy."

"Why?" asked Kaitlin. "You believe in ghosts?"

Glenn shook his head. "No. But I guess the thought of all those dead bodies psyches me out a little. Plus, I don't like to think about death."

"Everybody dies."

"I know." Then Glenn's expression turned mischievous, and he pulled her towards the woods. "Not today, though!" he exclaimed. They ducked through the bushes and between the trees. Every now and then he held a branch so it wouldn't snap back and hit Kaitlin in the face. She figured that at least was something to appreciate.

"You guys hang out here a lot, don't you?" Glenn asked.

Kaitlin shrugged. "A bit. Michael and I used to play here, when we were kids." As soon as she said it, she wished she hadn't mentioned his name.

But Glenn just nodded. "I know he's your arch-enemy and all, but he seems like an okay guy."

Kaitlin just made a face.

"I hope I never get on your bad side!" he exclaimed.

"Well," said Kaitlin softly, "you'd better be careful then. Come on," she said. "I'll show you our favourite hide-and-seek spot." She pulled him by the hand through the trees to a clearing marked by massive grey rocks. "These were dumped here by a glacier in the ice age," she explained to Glenn.

He looked impressed. "Really?"

"I have no idea," she admitted sheepishly. "Maybe!"

They both laughed as if the remark had been terribly funny. Glenn climbed up onto one of the big rocks and reached down to pull Kaitlin up beside him.

She glanced at Glenn, but he was watching the clouds float by. "People always see rabbits when they look at clouds, but I've never even come across one decent rabbit," he said.

"What do you see, then?"

Glenn squinted at the sky, shrugging a bit. "A herd of fluffy sheep?" he suggested, sounding hopeful.

"That's not very imaginative!" she chided. "You

know, when I was young, I used to think that if I could only go in a plane, I could open the window and grab a piece of cloud. I always said I'd put it in a little bottle, to save for when I was back on the ground."

"You know, you strike me as the sort of girl who'd carry around a piece of cloud," he said, with a smile.

"What's that supposed to mean?"

But Glenn didn't answer. He just moved closer, with a purposeful look in his eye. Kaitlin could feel butterflies growing in her stomach. Glenn leaned very close and kissed her once, lightly on the mouth. He whispered to her, "That wasn't so bad, was it?"

And then he kissed her again, more slowly.

Kaitlin's heart was beating so fast. She was relieved to suddenly hear Tracy calling through the woods, but Glenn looked less than pleased.

"They're looking for us," she explained unnecessarily as she got up from the rock, unnerved by Glenn's intense gaze. She dashed down a small hill towards the voices.

"Hey, wait up!" Glenn protested. But she ran even faster. She was breathless when she broke back into the open graveyard. She expected to see Tracy and Chuck but was more than startled to nearly run into Michael.

He eyed her breathlessness a bit curiously. "Nice day for a run through the woods, Kaitlin?"

She scowled at him and turned away. But he stepped into her path. "Hey, wait. I came looking for you."

She blinked at him. She wondered if her face was totally flushed. Her mouth felt like it was burning.

"Don't look so surprised. My parents and yours want to go out together. They want you to come home and watch Anna, so I told them I could probably track you down."

Kaitlin nodded slowly, her thoughts racing.

Michael seemed to hesitate. Then suddenly he blurted out, "Do you want me to walk you home?"

"Oh, I've got that under control," said Glenn's deep voice, as he came out of the woods with Tracy and Chuck following. Glenn took Kaitlin's hand in his, rather possessively.

Michael's expression grew distant, although he just nodded. "You'd better hurry," he said to Kaitlin. His eyes looked cold.

She wanted to say something, but it felt like her tongue was in knots. Then Michael turned on his heel and strode away.

Fifteen

So," said Glenn, his eyes glinting at Kaitlin as he leaned over the computer monitor, "is it time to reel her in?" He was grinning in such an odd way that Kaitlin—seated in front of the computer—wondered if he were thinking about the graveyard.

There was a soft cough from Winter. "It's not too late to drop this," she whispered. Kaitlin exchanged a long glance with her friend.

"What?" shrieked Tracy. "Of course it's too late." She stood up, waving her arms about to stress her point. "Shelley is totally into Andrew; we've got to go ahead with the plan now."

Frowning at Tracy's interruption, Winter turned back to Kaitlin. "Not so. We could just turn off the computer today and never log on as Andrew again." She paused for a moment to let that sink in. "Of course, Shelley would wonder what had happened, but she'd get over it."

Glenn laughed derisively. "You're losing your nerve, I think," he taunted, looming above Kaitlin.

"Bah. I'm just trying to think of the best way to make this work," Kaitlin explained, hating how defensive she sounded. "I want to somehow force Shelley to have to make a specific choice between doing something with Michael or going to meet Andrew."

Winter sighed and leaned back in her chair.

"How about scheduling the meeting during one of Michael's basketball games?" Glenn paused, thinking. "Say, we've got an important game next Friday night. And of course, Shelley the cheerleader is always on hand screaming her lungs out for Michael."

Chuck nodded sagely. "Yeah, if I was Michael, I'd be mad if she took off to meet some other guy, especially then."

Kaitlin pondered their words, and despite warnings from Winter, typed out a message to Shelley. In it, Andrew said he'd be in Shelley's part of town next Friday night, and would love to take her out—maybe about seven PM, meeting at the gates to the school? After incorporating some mushy emotional stuff as prompted by Tracy, Kaitlin sent the email.

Then both girls collapsed in fits of nervous giggles.

"Aren't computers amusing?" a voice inquired blandly behind them. Kaitlin swivelled fast in her chair to see Michael leaning against the doorframe, eyeing the group curiously. "Why do you waste your lunch hours in here, hmm?" His gaze travelled pointedly over the group.

"It's nothing to do with you, Michael!" Tracy shrieked out.

He raised an eyebrow at her. "Well, I'd certainly hope not."

Discreetly wrapping her fingers around Tracy's wrist,

Kaitlin squeezed out a warning to stay silent.

"There's plenty of computers for all," Michael added. "It seems such a big gang of you to crowd around just that one."

Glenn chuckled. "Don't forget, we like to stick very close to Kaitlin," he replied challengingly.

"Whatever," Michael drawled dismissively, but his expression was dark. He locked eyes for a long moment with Glenn. "Don't be late for practice tonight," he commanded quietly, before turning to leave.

"Yes, *sir*," Glenn replied, but Michael was already gone. He shrugged to pass off the moment. "I guess that was a close call."

"I guess so!" exclaimed Kaitlin, throwing an angry look at Tracy.

"What? What?" her friend protested. "I didn't do anything!"

Kaitlin sighed and rolled her eyes.

* * *

When Shelley's email response arrived the next day, it was full of excitement about the prospect of finally meeting Andrew. But she explained that next Friday evening was a really bad night, because of her cheerleading duties at an important game.

Kaitlin smiled grimly and wrote a tough reply coated in the most affectionate language. She asked Shelley to make a choice between meeting Andrew or hanging out at some basketball game.

They held their breath over the following day,

waiting for Shelley's answer. And it finally came.

> *Hi Andrew,*
>
> *It's going to be difficult for me to get away Friday night, but because I want to meet you so much, I'm going to arrange it. I'll meet you at the gates to the school at 7 p.m.*
>
> *You're so handsome and mature, I've been thinking about you all the time. I can't wait to see you in person. It would be so cool to date a guy in high school.*
>
> *XO*
>
> *Shelley*

Kaitlin and Tracy squealed in nervous delight. Kaitlin checked the room to make sure no one was lingering in the doorway, then she read out the note to the others in a low voice.

Chuck and Glenn whooped and did high-fives. Winter lifted her head from her history textbook and deliberately turned the page to continue with her reading. But she dropped the book altogether when she heard the room's printer come alive and spit out a piece of paper. "What are you doing?" she asked.

Kaitlin smiled triumphantly at her friend. "That's the evidence, of course!"

"We're going to give that to Michael," Tracy interjected eagerly.

Winter clasped her hands to her brow. "Heaven help us," she murmured.

*   *   *

The plan was fairly simple. While Shelley was waiting by the gate for Andrew to show up, Michael would be inside the school playing basketball. At some crucial point, he'd receive the note detailing Shelley's betrayal.

Kaitlin decided it would be best for Glenn to slip the note somewhere that Michael would be sure to find it, because Glenn, as a member of the basketball team, would have ample opportunity. To her surprise, he protested vehemently when she proposed that he place the note. But Kaitlin and Tracy made comments about his lack of courage until he reluctantly gave in.

Along with the printed email from Shelley, Kaitlin had included a low-resolution printout of the photograph that the girl had sent to Andrew. Kaitlin also added a short, typed note.

Michael,
It seems you're not that appealing to your girlfriend.
In fact, she's more interested in a guy who doesn't even exist. See the nice photo she sent him? Too bad he's not going to show up to take her out. Too bad she's stuck with you.

She left the note unsigned.

Even Tracy gasped when she read it and said that it was too mean, but Kaitlin wasn't about to be deterred. She sealed the envelope and gave it to Glenn, who looked a bit pale as he tucked it into his pocket. But he leaned close and whispered into her ear: "See what I'm willing to do for you, Kaitlin?"

Kaitlin just mumbled something about how she appreciated the help.

Shelley didn't show up at the game. It was up to the rest of the cheerleaders in their blue and yellow uniforms to jump into the air and shout encouragement to the team.

Kaitlin discreetly took a seat at the back of the bleachers, along with Tracy, Chuck and Winter. There was quite a loud, boisterous crowd of students and parents. Despite the warmth of the room, Kaitlin kept shivering. As the guys warmed up, the loud pounding of the bouncing basketballs and squealing running shoes reverberated throughout the gym and even more loudly in her head. She watched as Michael darted about, dribbling and passing the ball to his teammates.

Soon, the game was neck-in-neck between the home team and the visiting rivals. It was clear that Michael was a star player and a favourite with the crowd. Glenn wasn't doing badly either, Kaitlin reminded herself.

At half-time, Kaitlin watched as Michael approached the bench, flushed from his exertions. When he picked up his towel to wipe off his forehead, Kaitlin gasped as the note tumbled to the floor. Then she held her breath, because Michael hadn't even noticed. The note slid off the shoe of a guy walking past with a water bottle and floated nearly under the bench. In an instant of panic, Kaitlin reversed her wishes and prayed that the note would stay hidden.

But one of his teammates saw the envelope and picked it up curiously. He turned it over and, seeing Michael's name on the front, handed it over.

Michael tore it open. He sat down on the bench and flipped through the pages, his gaze resting for a long moment on the photo printout. He turned back to the other two notes and read each again. He glanced quickly at the crowd, his eyes searching it for just a moment. Throwing down his towel, Michael leapt up, said something to the coach and dashed out the side door of the gym. In the rush, his shoulder bumped Glenn's with such force that the other boy went sprawling to the ground. Glenn rubbed his arm angrily and threw a fierce look up towards his friends in the bleachers. The coach went over to help him up, but Glenn irritably shrugged him off.

Tracy and Kaitlin stared at each other, wide-eyed. "Come on!" shrieked Tracy, grabbing Kaitlin's hand. They ran upstairs to a window in the hallway which overlooked the front of the school.

The sun had set, but the schoolyard was still relatively bright, thanks to an abundance of outdoor lamps. They arrived in time to see Michael approaching Shelley. The girl jumped up from her seat on the curb in visible alarm.

Although the watchers couldn't hear what was being said, Michael now appeared fairly calm as he walked up to the gate, still holding the letter. He handed all the pages to Shelley, who read them slowly. Then she seemed to crumple to the ground. She buried her face in her hands, and her shoulders were shaking.

Kaitlin realized that the girl was crying.

Michael watched dispassionately from a distance as Shelley rose and took a step towards him. He shook his head firmly at her. They spoke for a few moments, then, still crying, she ran into the school.

Kaitlin's heart felt like it was pounding out of her chest, and her stomach was turning over rapidly. "I feel like I'm going to throw up," she whispered to Tracy.

"You have a nervous stomach," Tracy said, her eyes still fixed on the schoolyard.

Michael just stood there for what seemed like a very long time.

Kaitlin pulled back into the shadows as he turned to look at the school, but not before she caught a glimpse of the very dark, angry expression on his face. She took a deep breath and hissed at Tracy, "I don't know about you, but I'm leaving now."

Tracy nodded. "Better take the back way out."

*   *   *

Kaitlin tiptoed about all weekend, half-expecting to see a furious Michael appear on her porch at any moment. But there was no sign of him.

Then again, she told herself, there was no reason to believe he knew of her involvement in Shelley's betrayal. She half-wanted him to know how she'd gotten back at him but was afraid of the consequences. She wondered if Michael was very upset at losing Shelley.

But if he were hurt, so much the better, she told herself firmly. She wondered why she didn't feel more triumphant about her success. She had a hollow feeling in the pit of her stomach that she tried to suppress, concentrating instead on the fact that she'd achieved her revenge.

When Monday morning came, it was a rather quiet Kaitlin who trekked off to school. She didn't even have much to say when Audrey ran up to their lockers to excitedly share the news that Shelley and Michael were no longer "an item."

"Is that so?" said Winter coolly. "Very interesting, I'm sure." And she opened her locker, paying studious attention to the covers of her notebooks.

But Tracy was more interested in gauging the scope of the school gossip. "Really!" she exclaimed encouragingly to Audrey. "How do you know?"

Audrey tilted her head, a bit abashed. "I heard some of the Grade Eight girls talking about it in the washroom."

"Why did they break up?" Tracy inquired, while Kaitlin wordlessly rearranged textbooks.

"I don't know. But it happened during the basketball game. Michael actually left for a while in the middle to break up with her. Can you believe it?" Audrey's tone was one of gleeful astonishment.

"That must have been traumatic," Kaitlin commented, without looking at Audrey. "I guess he couldn't go back to the game?"

"That's the weirdest part! He went back and played like a maniac." Audrey smiled brightly. "Our team won hands-down, mostly thanks to Michael."

"Well, I'm sure he must still have been upset," said Tracy. "Now he doesn't have a girlfriend."

Audrey giggled as she walked away. "Oh, I bet there will be a lot of volunteers! He's so dreamy."

Kaitlin scowled. She nearly jumped at the sound of a deep male voice right behind her. She spun around expecting the worse, but it was only Brad. She stared at him suspiciously, because it wasn't like him to hang out around mere seventh graders.

But Brad appeared more than comfortable. He leaned against the lockers between Kaitlin and Winter, glancing back and forth between them. "My, my, Kaitlin," he said, his gaze finally settling on her. "So you've been messing around with Michael's life, have you?" he asked blandly.

Kaitlin took a nervous step backward. "I don't know what you're talking about," she said, trying to control the tremor in her voice.

Brad raised an unbelieving eyebrow at her. "You don't know that I'm talking about how you invented a guy and persuaded silly Shelley to fall for him?"

Kaitlin swallowed carefully. "Is that what Michael thinks?" she asked, raising her eyes to meet his.

Brad smiled darkly at her. "It's what Michael knows," he corrected. He glanced out of the corner of his eyes at Winter, who was leaning against her own closed locker with her arms crossed, listening. "It's actually pretty funny that you managed to do it." Then he cracked a grin in Kaitlin's direction. "You know what's really amusing?"

Kaitlin shook her head cautiously.

"You actually helped Michael out," Brad said.

That wasn't what Kaitlin had expected to hear. "What do you mean?" she said in confusion.

"She's too clingy. Michael wanted to get rid of her but didn't know how, because he didn't want to hurt her feelings. You made it easy for him."

Kaitlin could feel the blood rushing to her face. "It's not true," she gasped, staring at him. Then, more firmly than she'd intended, she slammed her locker door shut and faced him. "It's not true," she stated, daring him to argue.

But Brad only laughed. "I told you it's amusing," he said and shrugged at her before turning his attention to Winter. "Now what really perplexes me is your involvement. It doesn't seem your style."

Winter gave a short, low laugh and eyed Brad carefully. "Don't presume to know my style," she warned softly.

"Actually, Winter," Brad said, leaning closer, "all I expect from you are surprises." Then, turning his back completely on Kaitlin, he seemed to hesitate. Finally, he blurted out: "Listen, I'm going rollerblading after school. Do you want to come along?"

Winter tilted her head in Brad's general direction. "Only if you think you can keep up." She turned and strode off to class.

*   *   *

It wasn't until much later in the day that Kaitlin finally came face-to-face with Michael in a school stairwell. His expression was unreadable as he silently blocked her path. She moved to dart around him, but he shook his head at her. "No," he said, "stay a while."

Kaitlin opened her mouth to protest, but no sound came out. Her heart was beating quickly as she realized how angry Michael was. He stood very close, looking down at her. "All right, Kaitlin," he said in a firm but controlled manner. "Listen up. I know I hurt your feelings when I didn't let you play catch with the guys, but that was years ago. I don't know how many times I've apologized, but you'd never let it go."

He took a deep breath. "Basically, you let me know you don't want me involved in your life any more. Fine. I'm good with that." He paused. "Now I want the same from you."

He stood back, his piercing stare fixed firmly on her face. "Stay out of my life, Kaitlin," he ordered grimly. Then he turned and walked away. She struggled to think of something to yell at him, but nothing clever or sufficiently hurtful sprang to mind.

She couldn't understand why she felt like crying.

Sixteen

Moving through a bunch of rambunctious fifth-graders, Kaitlin carefully balanced her cafeteria tray, replete with hamburger, fries and root beer. She made her way over to her regular table, where Tracy and Winter had already taken their typical spots. Chuck and Glenn had yet to arrive.

Her tray clattered against the fake wood table as she slid in beside Tracy. "Hey, there," said Kaitlin.

"Yo," said Winter with a grin.

Tracy skipped the greeting altogether. She leaned over to Kaitlin and whispered, "She's still watching you."

Kaitlin's eyes flickered involuntarily to the table of Grade Eight girls that Shelley once again frequented since the fallout with Michael. "No," she protested nervously, "she's not watching me." Then she whispered a bit uncertainly to Winter, "Do you think she's watching me?"

Leaning back, Winter glanced over her shoulder at the other table. "Yep," she said, chewing on a carrot stick.

"Do you really think she knows we were being Andrew?"

"Oh, yeah. She knows."

Kaitlin conceded that the girl was pointedly glowering

in her direction. Squirming, she murmured defensively, "She should thank me for getting her away from Michael."

"Uh-huh," responded Winter, now deeply engrossed in a celery stick.

"Look, there's Chuck and Glenn," Tracy pointed out, elbowing Kaitlin, who shrugged but smiled at Glenn.

That's when Shelley made her move. As the boy passed, she called out his name. "Oh, Glenn," she said sweetly, "why don't you come sit with us today? We never get to chat."

Looking a bit startled, he glanced over at the Grade Seven girls, but Kaitlin quickly looked down at her plate. After just a moment's hesitation, Glenn sat down beside Shelley.

Chuck paused uncertainly, with a lost look on his face. Finally, he walked on and sat beside Tracy. "Sheesh." He shook his head. "A table full of Grade Eight women. Lucky Glenn."

Tracy kicked Chuck hard under the table. "Ow!" he protested defensively. "I didn't do anything! What?"

Kaitlin just kept her eyes on her plate.

"I can't believe it," gasped Tracy. "Shelley's going to try to steal your boyfriend, Kaitlin!"

Kaitlin flushed a bit. "He's not my boyfriend."

Tracy didn't seem to notice, but continued to rant. "You're going to have to do something, Kaitlin," she said. "Go get him!"

Winter chuckled. "That would be something to see."

Tracy was vehement. "You can't just let her steal away your boyfriend."

"He's not my boyfriend," Kaitlin repeated.

*　　*　　*

But just like that, Glenn's attentions shifted. He sat with Shelley and her friends at lunch and walked her home after school. The pretty blonde girl was even seen gripping his elbow on occasion. She seemed to take great pleasure in smiling triumphantly in Kaitlin's direction. Glenn, on the other hand, deliberately avoided eye contact with her.

Kaitlin didn't know what to think. Whether or not she'd actually wanted Glenn as a boyfriend was one matter. Who said she even wanted a boyfriend? But still, having Glenn lose interest felt decidedly unpleasant. But it was important not to give Shelley any more satisfaction from her conquest. She held her face in a calm, unconcerned expression whenever the couple was about.

But Tracy was furious and refused to speak to Glenn. Even her ardour for Chuck seemed to cool. One day when Glenn and Chuck were passing by the girls' lockers, Tracy reached out and grabbed Glenn's arm. "Just tell me," she demanded, "what do you think you're doing with Shelley, hmm? You were as much a part of the Andrew thing as any of us." She glared at him accusingly.

Glenn glanced at Kaitlin, who seemed engrossed in looking something up in the back of her science textbook. "I know that," he said simply. "I didn't know this would happen."

To Kaitlin's surprise, Winter stepped close to Glenn and said quietly, "You do know she's just using you to get back at Kaitlin, right?"

"Yeah, I guess I know that," he said, sounding a bit sheepish.

"So…" Winter paused, for emphasis. "Why?"

Glenn stared at Winter for a moment. "Well," he said, stumbling a bit over his answer. "I guess it's good, while it lasts." He hesitated, looking at Kaitlin.

Finally, Kaitlin turned and tossed her hair. "I'm so happy for you. Go enjoy yourself." She ground out the words coldly.

"Kaitlin…" said Glenn.

"*Now*," she said more loudly, "go now."

He looked at her a moment longer, sighed and obeyed.

Kaitlin threw her science book in the bottom of her locker with considerable force.

"I guess you girls are mad at him, eh?" Chuck observed cheerfully.

But then the unexpected happened. "You too!" cried Tracy. "You go away too!"

Chuck blinked in surprise. "I didn't do anything," he protested.

"I don't want you hanging around any more!" Tracy shouted, to everyone's astonishment. "Get away from me!"

Chuck flushed right to his hair roots. His expression turned sullen. "Fine," he answered angrily and stalked away.

Tracy slid to the floor beside her locker with tears streaming down her face. Kaitlin and Winter exchanged looks of shock and amazement.

"Tracy," gasped Kaitlin, "why did you say that to

Chuck? It doesn't matter about Glenn. It's not Chuck's fault."

Winter nodded, bending down beside Tracy. "I'll go get Chuck. You can tell him you're sorry, and I'm sure everything will be okay."

"No!" shrieked Tracy, grasping Winter's arm. "Don't! I don't ever want a boyfriend."

"You don't have to have a boyfriend if you don't want," Winter returned reasonably. "Or, at least wait until you're older. But you can be friends with Chuck."

Tracy shook her head violently. "I never want a boyfriend." And her shoulders shook with sobs.

Sliding down to the floor beside her friend, Kaitlin gently touched her on the shoulder. "Why don't you ever want a boyfriend?"

"There's no point," said Tracy, lifting her tear-filled eyes to Kaitlin. "Even if we fell in love and got married, we'd just end up divorced and miserable." She took a deep breath, hiccuping on a sob. "There's just no point," she whispered.

*   *   *

Kaitlin brought Tracy home with her after school. She'd stopped crying, but her eyes were strangely bright. She was talking really fast. "Don't you worry about Glenn," she chattered. "He wasn't worthy of you. So don't be upset. Don't worry."

Kaitlin blinked at her friend. "I'm not worrying." She shrugged demonstratively. "Whatever."

"That's right, that's the attitude. 'Whatever.' Don't

forget it, Kaitlin."

"Um, okay," agreed Kaitlin, staring in consternation at her hyper best friend.

"Here," said Tracy, suddenly shoving Fred into her friend's arms. "You can have Fred back."

Blinking, Kaitlin looked down at the small dog. She'd kind of missed her toy. "Why don't you want him any more?" she asked curiously.

Tracy just shrugged. "I'm bored of that, I guess. Hey, can we look in your garage?"

"Sure," said Kaitlin. "I guess so. Why?"

Tracy shrugged as Kaitlin turned on the garage light. "I just want to look. What's this?" Her voice raised a notch or two in excitement.

Kaitlin glanced to where Tracy was pointing. "You mean the wood?"

"Yes! The wood. What's it for?"

"I don't know. Probably nothing. Likely something left over from whatever my dad was last making."

Tracy's visage seemed to brighten. "Could I have it?" she pleaded.

"Why?"

Her friend looked irritated. "I just want it!"

"Do you want to build something?"

She nodded slowly. "That's right. I want to build something."

"What?" asked Kaitlin suspiciously.

Tracy sighed. "I haven't decided yet, okay?!"

"You'll have to ask my dad. It's his wood."

They found Kaitlin's father working in his den. "Mr. Anderson!" Tracy greeted exuberantly.

Kaitlin's father looked momentarily startled. But he laid aside his building plans and smiled at the girls. "Well, hello there, Tracy. How nice to see you!"

Tracy seemed eager to get the formalities over with. "Could I have a bit of your pile of wood?" she asked quickly.

Kaitlin's father looked confused. "Which wood?" He glanced at Kaitlin for an explanation.

"In the corner of the garage," murmured Kaitlin, still watching Tracy.

He followed them out to the garage to look at the woodpile. "Oh, right," he said, sounding a bit surprised to see it there. "How much did you want, Tracy?"

"Just a bit."

He nodded and laid aside a few pieces of wood.

"Could I have a bit more, please?"

"Oh," said Kaitlin's dad, seeing his now-treasured pile diminishing. "Sure. Here's a bit more. Is that enough?"

Tracy eyed her pile critically, then nodded. "That should be fine."

He resumed his jovial expression. "So, whatcha going to build?"

"That's what I wanted to know," said Kaitlin irritably under her breath.

"A chair," Tracy stated firmly. "I'm going to make a chair."

"Ah," sighed Kaitlin's father. "I'd like to make some chairs, but I don't have a lathe."

"It's not going to be that kind of chair," Tracy replied, almost belligerently.

Kaitlin's father just laughed. "Well, I wish you luck.

Maybe you can get Kaitlin interested in building too!"

"Fat chance," said his daughter. Tracy was staring at her newly acquired wood.

"I guess you're going to need a ride to get that home, Tracy," Kaitlin's father pointed out. "So just let me know when you're ready to go."

"I'm ready now," she said firmly.

"Oh, nice visit," Kaitlin commented.

*   *   *

The next day, when Tracy didn't show up at school, Kaitlin wasn't particularly concerned. But an odd feeling nagged at the back of her neck. And even though she'd managed to squeak by Winter on the latest science test, she couldn't shake a general feeling of unease. Then again, Kaitlin complained to herself, with Glenn's defection, Shelley's hostility and Michael's coldness, this was no time for a best friend to disappear.

But when Tracy still didn't come to school the following day, Kaitlin started to worry. Winter too expressed concern. "Let's stop by there after school to check on her," she suggested.

Kaitlin nodded slowly. "She might not want visitors if she's sick, though."

Winter shrugged. "We won't stay, then. We'll just peek in to check on her." That seemed like a good plan.

The nagging feeling grew as they approached Tracy's house. There were two cars in the driveway, so Winter pointed out that somebody must be home.

Kaitlin nodded slowly. "Her dad and her mom.

Something's going on," Kaitlin said.

Winter shrugged philosophically. "Well, all we can do is knock," she said. After a moment, Tracy's father answered the door. He ran his hand through his thinning hair and stared at the girls as if finding them on his doorstep was a complete surprise.

"Don't be a idiot," snapped Tracy's mother from behind. "Let them in; maybe they can help." Her makeup was still perfectly in place, but her look was harried.

"Oh, of course," he said finally and stepped back. "Come in, girls." He gave them an apologetic smile.

Kaitlin peered into the house. "Really," she explained hesitantly, "we just came to check on Tracy, because she wasn't at school today." She paused as soon as she'd said that. If Tracy had been playing hookey or something like that, Kaitlin hoped she wasn't getting her friend into trouble. But her parents didn't seem at all surprised.

Tracy's mother nodded impatiently. "She's upstairs in her bedroom." There was something odd about the woman's tone, as she glanced at her husband. "Why don't you girls go on up and ask her if you can go in and visit?"

Winter raised an eyebrow in Kaitlin's direction, but both girls nodded then climbed the stairs. To their surprise, Tracy's parents followed, although they hung back a bit, lingering near the bottom of the stairs.

Kaitlin knocked lightly on Tracy's door. There was no answer. She banged with a bit more force and called out: "Tracy, are you in there? It's Kaitlin and Winter."

There was a momentary silence inside before Tracy finally answered. Her voice seemed strangely muffled and distant. "I'm in here," the words wafted through.

Kaitlin frowned a bit and tried the door handle. It didn't budge. "Can we come in?" she called out.

"No!" shouted Tracy emphatically. Then after a moment, she said something else in a lower voice about nails. Kaitlin shook her head perplexedly. "What did she say?"

Winter just shook her head. "I didn't make it out either."

"She said," said Tracy's mother brittly, as she walked upstairs, "that you can't go in, because she's nailed the door shut!"

Winter and Kaitlin just stared at the woman, speechless. Kaitlin thought guiltily of her father's wood. Finally, Winter asked, "How long has she been in there?"

Tracy's mother threw an irritated glance at her husband. "We don't know for certain, but it's been at least two days." To the girls' surprise, she suddenly began pounding full-force on the door. "Sweetie! Let me in! I want to see you. We can talk about whatever the problem is. Open up! Open this door right this instant!"

There was no response from within. Tracy's mother collapsed against the doorframe. Her husband patted her arm awkwardly. "Now, Lilith," he said quietly, "you know we've already tried that."

"Maybe she'll come out when she gets hungry, or needs to use the washroom?" Winter suggested hopefully.

"She's got a bathroom in there," Kaitlin reminded Winter in a whisper.

Tracy's mother's eyes filled with tears. "It's called an en suite, dear..." she said. Her words trailed off helplessly.

Winter stepped up to the door and knocked. "Tracy,

it's Winter. Are you okay? Are you hungry?" After a minute, another muffled response came through the door. Kaitlin's brow crinkled as she tried to understand.

"She says she's got food," Tracy's father interpreted wryly.

The girls stared awkwardly at the adults. "I guess we should go," Winter said finally.

Kaitlin nodded in agreement. But she went over and knocked on the door again. "Phone me when you come out, Tracy!" she yelled. There was no response from inside. Both girls called out goodbye, but Tracy didn't answer.

"Thanks for coming," Tracy's father said. Her mother nodded.

"I'm sure she'll be out soon," Winter said. They nodded, as if they wanted to be convinced.

* * *

Kaitlin moped about her house, thinking she should have tried harder to find out why Tracy wanted that wood.

When the phone rang, Kaitlin was delighted to hear her best friend's voice. "Tracy!" she exclaimed, cradling the phone against her ear.

"Shush," the girl cautioned. "Don't say my name. I don't want anyone to know I've got a phone in here. I took my dad's cell phone. I don't think he knows."

"You haven't come out of your room?"

"No," said Tracy quietly, her voice low. "I'm never coming out."

Kaitlin frowned slightly into the phone. "Why are you doing this?"

"I'm just tired of everything. I just want to stay in my room, that's all."

"Hmm," said Kaitlin, not really understanding. "Isn't it boring?"

"Well," Tracy conceded softly, "a bit. But I sleep a lot, and I have magazines in here. I even brought in a TV."

"It sounds boring," Kaitlin said. She cleared her throat. "So how much food do you have?"

Tracy's sudden laughter rang eerily out over the phone line. "I think I have a couple of months' worth of cans in here. Don't forget I do the shopping now." She paused. "Or I did. Do you think my dad will buy his own groceries now?" She actually sounded concerned.

"I don't know why not. My dad buys groceries sometimes."

"Oh!" added Tracy. "My mom's been over every day banging at my door!"

"I think she feels bad that you won't come out."

"Good," retorted Tracy defensively. Kaitlin could hear some static on the line, and it sounded like Tracy was moving about the room. "Listen, I've got to go. They're coming back upstairs. But hey. I just wanted to ask you one thing."

"Yes?"

"Did Anna like those brownies?"

Kaitlin eyes flew open. "You!" she gasped. "That was so creepy. Why did you do that?"

There was a long pause. "I just wanted to make Anna happy," Tracy said, a bit wistfully. There was a long pause. "She was happy, wasn't she?"

"Yes..." Kaitlin responded slowly.

"I gotta go," Tracy said, her voice breaking slightly. She hung up.

*　　*　　*

After three days, the word got out. Neighbourhood children gathered on the front lawn of Tracy's house to stare at it and whisper about the girl boarded up inside. They'd often yell out suggestions about how to get her to come out. The favourite suggestion seemed to be chopping down the door with an axe or a chainsaw.

Kaitlin was surprised to find Chuck standing there one day, looking mournful. "I just want to see her," he confessed sadly. "Do you think she's in there because she's mad at me?"

Kaitlin shook her head. "I don't think it's about you at all, Chuck."

"Do you think she misses me?"

"I don't know." She sighed and walked , leaving him standing there.

*　　*　　*

The next day, as Kaitlin was walking home from school, a fire truck rolled down the road. Following her intuition, she started to run after it. Sure enough, it was parked in front of Tracy's house. A large crowd began to gather. Tracy's parents were out on the lawn talking with a couple of the firefighters. Her father pointed up at Tracy's third-floor bedroom, and the firefighter nodded. They took a big ladder off the truck, leaned it against the side of the house and climbed it.

The man tapped lightly on Tracy's window. Then to Kaitlin's astonishment, he took off his firefighter's hat, and long, curly blonde hair tumbled out. She gasped.

After a few moments, he pushed open the window and climbed in. He took a seat on the windowsill, his back towards the onlookers. He must have been talking to Tracy, because he didn't move from his seat for a very long time. But eventually, he got up and disappeared into the room.

The crowd waited breathlessly.

When the firefighter appeared at the doorway to the house, a cheer went up from the kids and neighbours gathered on the lawn. Tracy's father shook the young man's hand briefly, then disappeared back into the house. The other firefighters briskly gathered up the ladder to load it back onto the truck.

Kaitlin stared at the man as he walked towards her. "Terry!" she breathed. "What are you doing dressed as a firefighter?"

He grinned at her. "I *am* a firefighter. A volunteer firefighter."

"I thought you were a philosopher."

"Hey, no point in limiting myself." He reached into the truck and pulled out a can of root beer. He handed it to her.

Kaitlin accepted it, holding it close to her. She almost told him she'd saved the last one he'd sent over but stopped herself just in time. "Is Tracy okay?" she asked finally.

"Sure, she's fine. It's probably not a good time to see

183

her, though; she'll be talking to her parents for a while, I think."

Kaitlin nodded.

"So, how's the revenge going that Tracy told me about?"

Kaitlin sighed. "We did it."

"And?"

"It wasn't as great as I'd hoped."

Terry smiled sympathetically. "You know," he shared, "the thing about grudges and revenge is that it's easy to just end up hurting yourself. Holding on to that stuff eats away at one's insides."

"Did you learn that in philosophy class?"

"I wish. Unfortunately, it was from life experience." He dramatically clapped a hand to his heart. "Think about it though, okay?"

"Okay."

The other firefighters were calling for Terry. He climbed up on the back of the truck. "Hey, guys," he said, "this is my friend Kaitlin."

Immediately they all started waving and calling her name.

The other kids were staring at her enviously as the truck pulled away.

Seventeen

On Sunday afternoon, Tracy came over to Kaitlin's house. She looked a bit sheepish as she greeted Kaitlin's father and Jane, but they just smiled kindly at her and asked her how she was doing.

"Better, I guess."

Jane nodded. "Good. And Tracy, if you're ever feeling bad, you can come talk to us, you know."

Up in Kaitlin's room, Tracy said she'd been very surprised when Terry appeared at her window. "I almost had a heart attack," she giggled. "And I was in my pajamas, and my hair was a mess!"

Kaitlin grinned sympathetically. "Were your parents very mad?"

"I think by that point they were just really glad I was out of my room! They talked about punishing me, but they didn't think sending me to my room made much sense!"

They both laughed.

"They took me to see a counsellor," Tracy confided. "I've got to go back regularly for a while." She brightened. "But my parents are both going to talk to the counsellor too."

"Do you think they'll get back together?"

"I don't know. Mom's still living in her own place, for now at least. The counsellor said I shouldn't get my hopes up too much. And if things don't work out between them, it doesn't mean that they both don't still love me. But..." Tracy leaned forward, whispering, "the three of us are going away for a weekend together!"

"That's pretty cool," Kaitlin smiled.

"Yeah. All I want is a real family all together like you have."

Kaitlin opened her mouth to protest at that. But suddenly, Anna started to pound on the locked door. The little girl shrieked loudly, demanding entry. "Some days they're too real, though!" Kaitlin remarked wryly.

Tracy giggled.

Later that afternoon, Kaitlin's father and Jane went out for a while. They asked Kaitlin to babysit her small sister and rake up at least some of the abundance of leaves covering the front lawn. "If you could gather at least a bag or so, it would be a great help, Katie," her father requested.

She didn't particularly mind. The air was brisk and cool, and the leaves crunched satisfactorily as she raked away at them. But just as soon as she had gathered a reasonable pile, Anna would run and throw herself on it, spreading the leaves and lessening the effectiveness of Kaitlin's toils.

Suddenly, Kaitlin glanced down at her wrist and felt her heart sink. The silver charm bracelet that her Gramma had given her wasn't there. She'd put it on earlier in the day, she knew, and it had been sparkling on her arm as she was raking. She let out a cry of alarm. "Anna! My bracelet, help me find my bracelet!"

The little girl scrambled over and eyed the ground ineffectively for about two seconds. "I don't see it!"

Kaitlin almost cried. Gasping in panic, she flattened the pile of leaves, searching through them for any hint of silver.

"Kaitlin," a voice spoke sharply to her. "What's wrong?"

Stricken, she looked up to see Michael's frowning face staring at her from the other side of the hedge. "I lost my mother's bracelet somewhere in the yard! I know it's here somewhere, but I can't find it!" Distress filled her voice.

He immediately bent down and slipped through the hole in the hedge. "Don't worry," he said gruffly. "We'll find it."

Together they searched across the lawn, through all the leaves. Eventually, Anna got bored and started to whine. She wanted to go watch TV, she said.

"Anna," said Michael firmly, "I want you to go swing on the porch swing. We're looking for something very important, and we need you to help us out by being very, very good. Maybe you can sing something to us."

To Kaitlin's amazement, Anna obeyed. She sat on the swing and bellowed out all her favourite songs. Every now and then Michael would compliment her on her singing, then she'd start a new rendition.

"Kaitlin," said Michael suddenly. She turned to look at him. He was reaching down beside the step to the porch. She cried out in excitement as she caught a glimpse of silver. She ran over to where he stood. Her bracelet was intact, lying against his palm.

Kaitlin's eyes filled with tears. "Oh, thank you," she said as he handed it to her. She zipped it securely into a jacket pocket, not trusting the bracelet's weak clasp again. "Thank you so much."

He nodded. "No problem, you're welcome." He stared at her for a moment, and she looked back at him uncertainly. "I'll be right back," he said and disappeared through the hedge.

A moment later he returned with a rake of his own. And he had a rake with a broken handle that was almost exactly the right size for Anna. The little girl was delighted.

Together, the three of them raked up the leaves. Kaitlin thought of telling Michael she only had to do a bag or two, but for some reason she didn't want the moment to end. Eventually, not one leaf remained on the lawn.

Michael wiped his brow. "I had no idea you guys had so many trees over here," he said, but he was smiling.

Kaitlin took a deep breath. "Do you want to come in for a drink?"

"Sure," he agreed readily.

Kaitlin got Anna settled with juice and cookies in front of the TV, then sat down across from Michael at the kitchen table.

"It was nice of you to help me."

"Oh well, just being neighbourly."

Kaitlin hesitated. "I...I'm sorry."

He looked startled. "What are you sorry for?"

"For...the stuff with Shelley."

"Ah," he said quietly, looking down at his hands. "I

felt bad for you when I saw her go after Glenn then." He lifted his head and looked at her earnestly. "Are you very upset?"

Kaitlin shook her head slowly. "He wasn't my boyfriend, you know."

"I wasn't sure. I'm glad to hear it, though." He smiled at her. "So," he raised an eyebrow, "in the future, if you object to my friends, or anything I'm doing for that matter, maybe you could come to me, and we could talk about it?"

She felt her face grow red. "I won't set any more imaginary friends on you."

"That's a relief." He grinned, but then his face turned serious. "Kaitlin?"

"Yes?"

"Do you think we could be friends again?"

She felt her heart beat very fast, but in a good way. "If we both want that, I think so."

"It's what I want," he said firmly.

She took a deep breath. "Me too."

*   *   *

The air was definitely cool. Almost all the deciduous trees had dropped their leaves, and there was a certain feeling in the wind, heralding the impending change of season.

Kaitlin couldn't wait to get home from school. She raced down the school steps and down the sidewalk as fast as she could, her open jacket streaming behind her. Suddenly, Michael raced up beside her. He bent over a bit, taking deep breaths of autumn air. "I thought I was

189

supposed to be the athletic one," he protested, grinning. "You definitely should join the track team! What's the hurry?"

"Gramma's coming to visit!" Kaitlin told him, almost shyly.

"Oh, she's such a great lady. I've always been jealous of you for having her!"

"And she seems to think of you as some sort of grandson, I think."

Michael seemed pleased.

Sure enough, Gramma's big black car was sitting in the driveway. "Well," said Michael, glancing at Kaitlin, "I guess I'll see you later."

He was already walking towards his own house, when Kaitlin said, "Don't you want to come in and say hello?"

"I was hoping you'd ask!"

They both smiled.

"Gramma!" Kaitlin shouted eagerly as she opened the door. The older woman appeared as quick as a flash and enveloped Kaitlin in a tight hug.

"It's my wonderful granddaughter. And that nice boy Michael! It's good to see you, son!" She beamed at them both.

If Jane or Kaitlin's dad were surprised to see Michael invited into the house, neither mentioned it.

"Here, here," bustled Gramma. "Candy for everybody." She handed a bag to the new arrivals. Anna was already sucking contentedly on a strand of green licorice.

"Aw, Gramma," said Michael, "you don't have to give me anything."

"Nonsense! I brought that for you. This just means

I don't have to send Kaitlin over there to get you!"

"Actually, feel free to do that," Michael teased, with a glance towards Kaitlin. She scowled, then smiled.

Later, Kaitlin and her grandmother sat on the porch swing. "I told you he was a nice boy, didn't I?"

"Gramma!" Kaitlin protested.

The older woman leaned back, well pleased. She squeezed Kaitlin's hand.

The door opened, and Jane carried out a cup of hot chocolate for each of them. "The air's getting a bit chilly; I thought this might help." She glanced at Kaitlin. "You can borrow my jacket just inside the door if the one you've got on isn't warm enough."

"Thanks, Jane," Kaitlin smiled, "but I'm warm enough for now."

Her grandmother, who was almost always polite, coolly thanked Jane for the hot chocolate. She stared down at it almost suspiciously after the younger woman had left.

Kaitlin gently placed a hand over her grandmother's. "Gramma?"

"Yes, dear?"

"Do remember how you told me you were nice to Anna because she's my sister?"

"Of course. I hope you're not upset about that. I think it's important for me to care for your sister too."

Kaitlin nodded slowly. "What about Jane?"

"What's that, dear?"

"Don't you think it's important to be nice to Jane?" Kaitlin asked carefully.

"Jane's not your mother," Gramma retorted sharply.

Kaitlin nodded, folding and unfolding her hands in her lap. "See...the thing is, I wish so much that my mother was here. But, she's not." She paused. "Jane's the closest I have to a mother, and she tries very hard, and...I think she loves me."

"Of course," Gramma replied automatically. "You're very lovable." But she fell silent, as if she were thinking about what Kaitlin had said.

*   *   *

The next day, Jane literally started to choke when Gramma complimented her on her pot roast. Then, when Gramma invited her to play a game of checkers, Jane seemed shocked. Gramma won the first game, but Jane won the second. "You've got a very talented wife, Daniel," Gramma said. They both just gaped at her before he recovered his wits and stammered a reply.

Later, Kaitlin curled up with her Gramma on the sofa. "Thank you," Kaitlin whispered.

"Whatever for?"

"For being extra-nice to her, of course."

"Bah, I don't know what you're talking about," said Gramma. But she smiled and squeezed her granddaughter's hand.

*   *   *

"Kaitlin!" Jane called up the stairs. "The door's for you!"

Kaitlin hadn't been expecting any visitors, but she dashed downstairs, then stopped short when she saw a grinning Michael leaning against the doorframe. "Can you come out and play?"

She laughed aloud.

"Actually," he continued, "my mom sent me over to see if you want to do some painting at our place this afternoon."

"Walls or ceilings?" she asked innocently.

"She'd prefer we start on paper," he replied in mock-seriousness.

"We?" Kaitlin lifted an eyebrow. "I didn't know you liked to paint, Michael."

"I don't mind it; I'm just really bad at it," he said ruefully.

She followed Michael outside, and they slipped through the hedge into the yard next door.

Michael's mother had paper and paints already laid out for them.

Kaitlin and Michael painted with their papers flat on the kitchen table; Mrs. Drayson had a small easel set up beside them. She generally painted images of flowers and birds, along with the occasional muted landscape. She whistled softly as her brush moved across the paper, revealing a small sparrow flitting over daisies.

Kaitlin loved the feel of smoothly spreading paint and revelled in mixing the colours in new and interesting ways. This time she attempted a bright red rose in full bloom. She used dark red, purple and yellow paint for accents and shadows and defined the stem in three shades of green plus pale yellow. She was completely focussed as she worked, blocking out almost everything else around her. But when she finished, she got up and gazed in admiration at Mrs. Drayson's painting. "I wish I could do birds," she said mournfully.

Mrs. Drayson only smiled, absently brushing a strand of hair away from her face with the back of her hand. "It just takes practice, dear."

Kaitlin squinted at Michael's page, which was full of indiscriminate colourful blobs. "What is it?"

"You mean you can't tell?"

Kaitlin stared in consternation. She didn't want to hurt his feelings, but she honestly couldn't make out what was depicted in his painting.

Then he burst out laughing. "You should see the look on your face! It's not anything in particular, it's just an abstract."

"Oh," exclaimed Kaitlin, relieved. She added quickly, "Well, it's very nice, in any case."

"Hah!" he scoffed good-naturedly. "But Kaitlin, that's a great rose. I'm impressed."

Mrs. Drayson leaned over Kaitlin's shoulder to examine the painting. "Oh, it's wonderful! You've got such talent, Kaitlin."

Kaitlin flushed, grateful but embarrassed. She was spared from replying by the arrival of Mr. Drayson in the kitchen. His big voice boomed out: "Ho! What do we have here? It's all my favourite artists!"

He whistled in boisterous admiration of Kaitlin's rose. Then he stood for an extra long time looking at Michael's creation with a bland expression on his face. Finally, he clapped his son on the shoulder. "My boy, that's the finest elephant I've ever seen!"

Mrs. Drayson and Kaitlin burst out laughing. But

Michael kept a straight face and nodded in grave acceptance of the compliment. "Thanks, Dad, I was hoping you'd be pleased!"

"Now, what I like," Michael's father said, "is finger-painting." He sat down in front of a spare piece of paper and stuck his index finger in some blue paint. His wife clucked at him as he quickly sketched a stick figure on his page. He held it up to Kaitlin for her inspection.

"Um, lovely!" she giggled.

He nodded solemnly. "Do you recognize who it is?"

"Is it Michael?"

"No, no. It's a self-portrait. It's the family resemblance that confused you."

Then he stuck his other index finger into green paint and drew another stick figure, adding a skirt in embellishment.

"Is it Mrs. Drayson?"

"Ah, lass, you're a connoisseur!" He used another finger for the red paint and began a third figure.

"Hey, Dad, I'm taller than that!" Michael protested.

"Yes, son," his father replied, "but you'll always be a wee lad in my eyes." He winked at Kaitlin. "What colour do you want to be, my dear girl?"

"Purple, of course!"

"Of course," he agreed affably and drew his last figure. "What a masterpiece," he crowed.

His wife pushed him toward the sink. "Wash your hands; you're a mess!"

They were all still smiling and joking as they cleaned up the paint and materials. Mr. Drayson stuck his finger-painting on the refrigerator door with a magnet.

Eighteen

Whispers and stares followed Tracy when she went back to class. Kaitlin could hear little snippets of conversations float around her, like "...she nailed herself in..." and "a firefighter climbed a ladder!"

"Just ignore them," Kaitlin whispered, annoyed. But Tracy looked pale. And Chuck was acting as some sort of self-proclaimed guardian, sticking closely to Tracy's side.

"For heaven's sake," exclaimed Winter, glancing around the cafeteria. Suddenly she leaned back in her seat and nearly shouted: "What a lot of effort just to get a couple of days off school, Tracy! Next time just fake a sore throat like the rest of us!"

Chuck burst out laughing. Then, seeing the humour, Kaitlin joined him. Finally, even Tracy broke out in a wide grin. Then an odd thing happened. Smiles and laughter erupted across the cafeteria.

After that, the comments seemed to die down. The opinion of the general student body soon swayed to a grudging admiration.

After lunch, Kaitlin slipped away to her locker. But a shadow suddenly fell across her path. "I need to talk to you," said Glenn in a low voice.

"Why? Isn't Shelley talkative enough?"

"Don't be mean. It doesn't suit you."

"What are you talking about? I'm known for my bad temper!"

Glenn sighed forlornly. "I never wanted to get on your bad side, Kaitlin. And I especially didn't want to hurt your feelings."

"My feelings weren't hurt. I don't care what you do."

"Don't act like that. I know you don't mean it."

Suspicion flashed through Kaitlin's mind. "Did Shelley dump you?" She thought she saw a guilty look flash across Glenn's face, but he covered it up quickly.

"We don't get along well," he explained evasively.

"So she did dump you."

"Remember how well you and I got along? Remember the fun we had?"

Kaitlin shrugged, thinking about the roller-blading fundraiser. "I suppose there was some fun," she conceded slowly.

"I just want it to be like that. I want to hang out with you and your friends, like we used to."

She stared at him for a long moment. "You can't go back. Nothing stays exactly the same."

Glenn suddenly grasped her hand. "Then be my girlfriend."

"What?" she gasped, truly shocked.

"I was crazy, I admit it. I like you so much, Kaitlin, I want you to be my girlfriend." His eyes shone fervently as he stared straight into her face.

Her emotions felt all awhirl. She swallowed hard, her eyes searching his face.

"Isn't this charming…" a deep voice drawled beside them. Michael's face was expressionless, but his eyes were distant and cold. "A happy reunion?"

"No," Kaitlin protested confusedly. She tugged at her hand, but Glenn wouldn't let go.

"That's right," he said to Michael challengingly. "It was happy enough before you showed up."

Kaitlin could feel the scorn in Michael's gaze as he said, "I'll get out of your way then."

"No!" Kaitlin called out after him as he strolled down the hall, but if he heard, he didn't look back. Exasperated, she tugged very hard and finally freed her hand from Glenn's. He looked at her in surprise. "Glenn, you can hang out with us if you want, and I'll be your friend." His face brightened. She quickly added, more firmly than she'd intended, "But I won't be your girlfriend."

"Why not?"

"Actually, I don't want a boyfriend," she said finally. When a flicker of hope sprang in his eyes, she quickly crushed it. "And if I did, it wouldn't be you."

"It's okay," Glenn said, at last. He turned and quickly walked away.

Kaitlin went in search of Michael.

Closing up his locker, he didn't look at her and spoke with what seemed like deliberate cruelty. "Why aren't you cooing with your new boyfriend, Kaitlin?"

"He's not my boyfriend! You misunderstood," she protested irritably.

"Listen, Kaitlin," said Michael coldly, "you don't have to explain to me."

"Michael Drayson, you cannot be mad at me!" Kaitlin shouted in her loudest possible voice at him.

He turned, lifting an eyebrow at her. "Oh?" he asked darkly.

She stared at him blankly for a moment. "Yes!" she yelled emphatically. "Because it's me who's mad at you!" She stalked away from him.

His hollow laughter echoed in the empty hallway.

Nineteen

Kaitlin drew her jacket up tight around her neck. The sky was unrelentingly grey, and the wind howled mercilessly, picking up leaves and pebbles and paper to pelt unsuspecting pedestrians. She shivered and hugged herself to keep warm.

"You had another fight with Michael?" Tracy asked, astonished.

Kaitlin shrugged as if she didn't care. "He was being an idiot."

"Is he your arch-enemy again?"

"Bah. He's not worth the effort." She tied the strings at the bottom of her coat more tightly.

"What about Glenn?"

"What about him?" Kaitlin adopted her best scowl. "I don't care about any of those boys."

The girls stared at each other wordlessly. "Brr, it will be winter soon," moaned Tracy. She jumped up and down a little, trying to keep warm.

"Bite your tongue," Kaitlin admonished, shoving her hands deep into her pockets. "But tomorrow I'm going to wear gloves." After a moment she added: "If I can find any, that is. I finished last winter with about six gloves, but no pairs!"

"Maybe Jane can tie each glove onto a string, like with little kids."

Kaitlin eyed her friend warily. "Don't suggest it! I bet she'd think it was a great idea!"

"Now I have something to hold over you!" Tracy teased, and they both giggled.

A car pulled up with a light honk of its horn. "I've got to go. They've been babying me, afraid of where I'll lock myself next, I think," said Tracy, a bit apologetically.

"You're not planning to do that again, are you?"

"Naw. You were right. It was pretty boring in there."

Kaitlin smiled. "I thought so!"

"Do you want a ride home?"

She shook her head. "Naw, I feel like walking for some reason."

"Are you sure? It's freezing out here!"

"You go ahead. Commune with your mother or whatever it is you do now." Kaitlin waved as Tracy ran off towards the car. Pushing her hands very deep into her pockets, she trudged home. The wind was so strong that she had to put some force into her walking, as if the air was suddenly extra-thick. She felt tears form in the corners of her eyes, stung by the cool breeze.

Reaching her neighbourhood, Kaitlin noticed that Mrs. Peters' face was pressed against the window, staring between a crack in the curtains. But it was the police car parked on the road that made Kaitlin's heart suddenly beat very fast.

It was right in front of her house.

She started to panic. What if something had happened

to her family? Suddenly oblivious to the cold, she ran as fast as she could towards home. The wind bit into her face and her lungs, but she didn't even notice.

She burst through the door and yelled for her father. There was a clatter from the other room. He came quickly around the corner.

"You're...not hurt?" she asked, almost frantically.

Her father shook his head, looking directly at her.

"What about Jane? And Anna? Is everybody okay?"

"Jane and Anna are in the living room. We're okay."

Kaitlin suddenly felt embarrassed and tried to catch her breath. "I guess it's silly," she gasped, "but I saw a police car outside, and I was worried that you guys were hurt." She smiled, half-apologetically, as she pulled her shoes off.

Her dad was still staring at her. He seemed very pale. "Kaitlin..."

Kaitlin felt as if a knife had turned in her stomach. "What's wrong, Dad?" she cried out.

"Come into the living room," he said.

Jane was sitting on the sofa. Her eyes were red, as if she'd been crying. Anna was quiet for once, staring at a cartoon on the television, but the sound had been turned off.

"What's wrong?" begged Kaitlin, unable to bear the sense of the dread weighing down on her.

"There was a car accident this afternoon," her father said slowly, his voice breaking. "Ben Drayson was killed, Katie." Kaitlin felt as if a huge hand had clamped around her windpipe. She couldn't breath. There was a roaring in her ears. She could hear her father's voice, but it sounded like it was coming through a long tunnel. "A drunk driver ran a red light. They think Ben was killed almost instantly." Her father's face looked strange. It seemed extra tight, as if it had been somehow stretched. He came over and laid a hand on her shoulder. "I've got to go over there, to help with some of the arrangements. I was just waiting for you to get home."

Kaitlin stared at him. He left, with just one backwards glance.

Jane started crying. Kaitlin crossed the space between them, and they hugged each other tightly. They sat there on the sofa for a long time without speaking.

But for once, Kaitlin couldn't cry.

Twenty

The air was thick but dry in the small room. An over-zealous heating unit buzzed softly, providing subtle background music to mix with the low murmurs of the hushed voices. The lingering scent of the flower bouquets on and around the polished casket wafted through the heavy air.

Kaitlin's father and Jane stopped to speak briefly with another couple from the neighbourhood. Kaitlin tugged at her tights, which were starting to droop around the ankles.

Anna gripped Jane's hand tightly. The room was packed with people: neighbours, relatives, friends and business colleagues. "A terrible tragedy...so young..." the voices whispered.

Mrs. Drayson's eyes were teary. She clutched a tissue in her hand as she hugged each person in Kaitlin's family and thanked them for coming. Michael stood stonily beside the casket. He shook hands when they were proffered, but his gaze was empty. His expression flickered for just a moment when Kaitlin's father squeezed him around the shoulders.

"Why is the casket closed?" Kaitlin whispered a few

minutes later to her dad. He hesitated, then said it was probably because Mr. Drayson had been in an accident.

Kaitlin couldn't help wondering what her neighbour looked like, if it was so bad that the casket had to be closed. She stared at the large framed photo amidst the flowers. Mr. Drayson's smiling face beamed back at her. She thought that smile seemed out of place now. Maybe someone should have looked for a photo with a more serious facial expression for such a solemn occasion.

She was surprised to see Winter and Brad at the wake. After a while, she followed them out to another room where coffee was being served, although none of them liked coffee. "I didn't think you knew Mr. Drayson," Kaitlin whispered.

"I didn't," Winter answered, "but I know Michael. My mom says wakes and funerals are for the living. It gives the people left behind a chance to grieve."

"I hate grieving," said Kaitlin.

Brad looked uncomfortable in a white dress shirt and tie. "Michael's really upset," he muttered. Kaitlin just stared at him. "I really liked Mr. Drayson. He was funny and always nice to me," he told them.

"He was nice to everyone," Kaitlin said flatly.

Winter glanced at the big clock on the wall. "We'd better go say goodbye to Michael. My mom's picking us up at eight." Then, she leaned over and whispered in Kaitlin's ear. "Chin up, girl. Don't forget Michael's going to need your friendship."

Brad followed her out of the room.

Kaitlin stood there for a long while, just staring at a poster advertising urns for cremation. She shivered.

Back in the other room, she took a seat by the back wall and watched the stream of people come and go. Mrs. Peters stood by the side of the room in her black funeral dress, sobbing loudly. Michael looked up, and his gaze met Kaitlin's. She swallowed and gave him a nod. He hesitated a moment, then nodded back before someone else came along to shake his hand and offer condolences.

It appeared that Jane had lost hold of Anna. The little girl came skipping into the room with a cube of sugar in her hand from the coffee tray. She popped it into her mouth. Immediately, her face broke out in a grimace.

"Just swallow it," Kaitlin ordered, afraid her sister would spit the offending item out onto the floor. Surprisingly, Anna obeyed.

"It tasted bad," she complained.

"I know. It's just sugar. It's not a candy."

"I thought it was a candy."

"Yeah, I did that once too, when I was little."

"Really?" Anna seemed pleased to hear that. She tilted her head consideringly at Kaitlin. "Can I sit on your knee?"

Kaitlin surprised herself by agreeing and gathered the child onto her lap. She wrapped her arms around her sister and squeezed the soft warm bundle.

"Is Mr. Drayson in the box or in heaven?" Anna suddenly whispered, sounding perplexed.

Kaitlin thought back to her Sunday School lessons. "I think his spirit is in heaven, it's just his body that's in the box."

"He needs his body in heaven." Anna looked worried.

"I think he gets a new one in heaven."

"A better one?"

"I guess so."

Anna seemed satisfied. Kaitlin held her tightly and stared at Mr. Drayson's photo. She could feel the tears pricking the corner of her eyes.

"Don't cry," Anna protested. "I'll tell you a secret." She took Kaitlin's hand in hers and squeezed it three times in rapid succession. "That's the secret," she said proudly.

Kaitlin squinted at her. "What's the secret?"

Anna squeezed her hand again, three times. She leaned close and whispered, "It means I love you."

Kaitlin felt a small burst of warmth in her heart. She nodded slowly and squeezed back, three times.

*   *   *

The car moved very slowly as part of the funeral procession on the way to the cemetery. Inside, no one said anything. Anna had been left with a babysitter for the rest of the day.

"You drove through a stop sign," Kaitlin pointed out, staring out the window.

"I know," said her father. "In a funeral procession, you just keep going."

She looked out the back window. Sure enough, all the other cars moved through the intersection without pausing. Drivers in the other direction seemed to be waiting patiently. "The other drivers don't get upset?"

"Most people know funeral processions have the

right of way. It's a well-known custom."

"I think it's even a law," added Jane very softly.

The car fell back into silence.

At the cemetery, people parked their cars and filed slowly towards the grave site. The road was covered in mud. "We should have worn boots," Jane murmured.

"It's mostly frozen," said Kaitlin's father.

The casket was covered with flowers from the funeral home. Reverend Brown spoke briefly. Mrs. Drayson clasped Michael's hand. His knuckles were white.

Kaitlin heard the low rumble of the minister's voice mix with the whispers of the chilling wind. She stared at the gaping hole below the casket, where the rich brown earth was exposed. When he closed his Bible and finished a prayer, the mourners shifted a bit, and some people even stamped their feet, trying to stay warm in the biting cold.

Mrs. Drayson was crying, pressing a shrivelled tissue to her face. She reached over and pulled a handful of roses from the top of the casket.

The crowd parted to let the family through.

Mrs. Drayson paused beside Kaitlin and wordlessly handed her one of the roses.

"Thank you," whispered Kaitlin.

The woman walked over the hard mud towards the road, but Michael stared at the rose in Kaitlin's hand. She gripped it tightly until a thorn started to dig into her flesh. He turned and looked back at the casket, until his mother quietly called his name.

Later, Kaitlin pressed the rose in a large book and locked it in her cabinet.

She didn't see much of Michael that next week. He didn't go to school, and the driveway seemed to be always full of vehicles owned by visiting relatives. By Friday afternoon, it looked like the guests had finally left. Kaitlin let herself into her house with her key, listlessly wandering about the empty rooms. At the side window, she stared at the house next door. Everything looked quiet.

Kaitlin picked up the phone and dialled Jane's office.

Jane sounded concerned. "Kaitlin! Is everything okay?"

"Yeah. I just wanted to say hi."

"Oh! Of course! How are you doing?"

"I'm okay. How are you?"

"I'm fine. So, what are you doing this afternoon?"

"Nothing. I just got home," reminded Kaitlin.

"Oh, right," replied Jane.

"Could I ask you something?"

"Of course!" Jane sounded surprised, but pleased.

"I'm thinking of going over to see Michael, but I don't know if I should. I don't want to bother them," she confided.

Jane didn't hesitate. "I think you should, yes. You don't have to stay long, but let Michael know you care. That's a good idea, Kaitlin."

"Okay. Thanks."

"No problem, Kaitlin! I'll be home in a couple of hours."

"Okay." She paused, then added, "Drive carefully."

There was a pause before Jane answered. "I will, I promise. See you soon."

"Bye, Jane," said Kaitlin. She hung up the phone and ran upstairs to get something out of her locked cabinet.

Hesitating just a moment, she tapped lightly on the heavy oak door. Mrs. Drayson opened it. Her hair had been pulled back into a bun, but several strands had escaped, giving her an overall untidy look. She held a paintbrush in one hand. "Come in, Kaitlin."

She followed Mrs. Drayson into the kitchen. The easel was set up and several paintings lay spread across the table. Unlike her usual pretty muted sketches, these were done in startlingly vibrant colours. Some paintings were of large vivid flowers, but most seemed to be more abstract; unidentifiable slashes and swirls.

Kaitlin just stared.

Mrs. Drayson laughed, almost nervously. "Don't tell me if you like them or not. This is just how I feel like painting right now."

"Okay," said Kaitlin. She looked at the refrigerator. Mr. Drayson's finger painting was still stuck to the door with a magnet.

"Did you come to see Michael?"

Kaitlin nodded.

"I was hoping you'd come by. He's downstairs." The woman dipped her brush in red and drew a dark slash across her painting. Kaitlin watched for a moment, then walked down the steep staircase leading to the rec room in the basement. Her hand glided lightly over the bannister. The wood felt cool under her skin. "Michael?" she called softly into the darkness.

"Kaitlin?" The light from a basement window shone dimly into the room. Sounding surprised, he looked up from where he was sitting on the floor, leaning against a sofa. His basketball was in his hands, and he dribbled it idly on the floor.

She sat down on the floor beside him.

"You know," said Michael, "whenever I did really well in a game, I used to always think how proud my dad was going to be of me."

"I think he was proud of you anyhow, though."

"Yeah."

Neither said anything more for a long time.

"Do you believe in heaven?" Kaitlin finally blurted out.

He looked at her. "I guess so. Yeah."

"Why?"

He shrugged expansively. "I don't know. Otherwise nothing makes sense."

"What do you mean?"

"Well, even if you look at the sky, or mountains or stuff like that. It doesn't make sense to me that it's there, if there's no God and no heaven," he said slowly. He turned to her. "Do you believe in heaven?"

"Yes," said Kaitlin.

"Why?"

She stared at the ceiling for a moment. "I have to believe it's true. Then I can see my mother again some day."

He nodded slowly.

"My mom wrote me a letter before she died."

"You never told me that."

"My dad just gave it to me a while ago. He saved it so I could read it when I was older."

"Wow," said Michael. "What did it say?"

Kaitlin touched the paper in her pocket lightly. "You can read it if you want," she offered hesitantly.

He stared at her for what seemed like a long while. "Okay." He set the basketball aside.

She carefully withdrew the letter from its envelope and handed it over. He seemed to read it very slowly, then stared at the page for a long time.

"My dad didn't have a chance to write a letter before he died," he said finally.

Kaitlin nodded, acknowledging the fact. "If he'd written, do you think he would have said he had a good life?"

"I guess so." He sighed.

"My mom said she wants me to tell her about everything she missed when I get to heaven," said Kaitlin thoughtfully. "I bet your dad will want to know about what you're doing too."

Michael nodded slowly.

She paused. "If I go to heaven before you do, I'll tell your dad all about what you've been up to, you know."

He smiled a bit at that. "I'll have to stay on your good side, I guess."

Kaitlin sighed. "I'm sorry for…"

He interrupted her, almost fiercely. "From now on, we're staying friends."

She nodded. "Okay."

"Even if we get angry sometimes."

"Okay," she repeated.

"Even if you're irritable."

She frowned.

"Even if you're being unreasonable."

She hesitated. "Glenn isn't my boyfriend, you know."

"Yeah?" said Michael. "That's good." He picked up his basketball again and just stared at it. His eyes were still rimmed with sadness.

Kaitlin got on her knees and wrapped her arms very tightly around him. He rested his forehead against her shoulder. She held him like that, for a long time.

"If I go to heaven first," he said finally, "I'll tell your mom all about you, Kaitlin."

Twenty-One

Kaitlin woke up to the sound of Anna shrieking. "Snow! Snow!" The little girl banged on her door, shouting happily. "Kaitlin! It's snowing! It's snowing! It's snowing!"

"Go away," mumbled Kaitlin from under her blanket. Her sister continued to dance around in the hallway, yelling delightedly about snow.

Kaitlin dragged herself out of bed and peered sleepily through her window. The ground was white. Big fluffy snowflakes danced slowly downwards outside her frosted windowpane. She couldn't help but smile at seeing it.

She dressed for school and went down for breakfast. "You're still here?" she asked her dad, surprised.

He smiled and nodded. "I'm slow this morning."

Gazing out the window, Kaitlin dreamily watched the snowflakes fall.

"You'd better get going if you don't want to be late like the rest of us," Jane said softly.

Kaitlin got up and kissed her dad's cheek, and then to everyone's astonishment, she kissed Jane. "I'm on a roll," Kaitlin told herself. So she kissed Anna, too.

"Eww!" the little girl protested. "Germs!"

Everyone laughed.

"Don't forget your new gloves," Jane reminded.

Kaitlin found the gloves in the hall cupboard. She held them in one hand as she went out the front door. A snowball bounced off her shoulder when she stepped off the porch.

"Hey!" she protested.

Michael stood in his yard. He slipped through the hole in the hedge. "We're going to be late," he accused, but he had a smile on his face.

"I didn't know you were waiting."

"Well. I had a hunch we might be going in the same direction."

"Oh," said Kaitlin. She felt happiness swell inside her as they walked together out of the yard.

He gave her a sidelong look.

"What?" she asked suddenly.

"I was wondering when you were going to put on those gloves."

"Why?" She glanced downwards, surprised to see that she was still carrying the new gloves.

"Because when you do, I'd like to hold your hand," he said simply, looking at her face.

So Kaitlin put on her gloves.

Grace Casselman has published primarily as a business and technology journalist, writing for a number of prominent newspapers, such as *The National Post, The Globe and Mail* and *The Calgary Herald*. She studied at Carleton University in Ottawa, where she earned an Honours Bachelor of Journalism. She is also the author of *Knocked Off My Knees: Coping When Chronic Illness Hits Hard* (PublishAmerica, 2003). She currently lives in Calgary, Alberta, with her husband and son. *A Hole in the Hedge* is her first book for young adults.